"Are you sure *it to my house?" Penny asked in a trembling voice.*

"Shame on you," Cabe said with a low, sexy chuckle. "Don't you know there's an unwritten code that says you never, ever insult a man's truck? Them's fightin' words, ma'am."

"Oh, sorry," she said. "This is the nicest truck I've ever ridden in."

"Yeah?" he laughed. "Could it be it's the only truck you've ever ridden in?"

"That's a mere technicality."

Cabe turned a corner then, and with a yelp, Penny was suddenly sliding across the seat, her arms and legs seeming to go in four different directions. Cabe flung out his arm and snagged her around the waist, hauling her close to his side.

"Hi, there," he said, dropping a quick kiss on her open lips. He kept his arm tightly around her as he came to a stop sign.

"No wonder men like trucks," Penny said breathlessly.

"They do have their uses," Cabe answered. "Now, you're supposed to drape your arm around my neck and put your head on my shoulder. There're rules about this pickup stuff, you know."

She began laughing as she followed directions to the letter. No question about it, she was putty in his hands. . . .

Bantam Books by Joan Elliott Pickart
Ask your bookseller for the titles you have missed.

WHAT ARE *LOVESWEPT* ROMANCES?

They are stories of true romance and touching emotion. We believe those two very important ingredients are constants in our highly sensual and very believable stories in the *LOVESWEPT* line. Our goal is to give you, the reader, stories of consistently high quality that may sometimes make you laugh, sometimes make you cry, but are always fresh and creative and contain many delightful surprises within their pages.

Most romance fans read an enormous number of books. Those they truly love, they keep. Others may be traded with friends and soon forgotten. We hope that each *LOVESWEPT* romance will be a treasure—a "keeper." We will always try to publish

*LOVE STORIES YOU'LL NEVER FORGET
BY AUTHORS YOU'LL ALWAYS REMEMBER*

The Editors

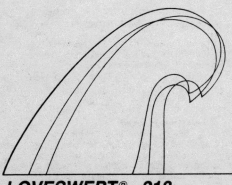

LOVESWEPT® • 218

Joan Elliott Pickart
Lucky Penny

BANTAM BOOKS
TORONTO • NEW YORK • LONDON • SYDNEY • AUCKLAND

LUCKY PENNY

A Bantam Book / November 1987

LOVESWEPT® and the wave device are registered
trademarks of Bantam Books, Inc. Registered in U.S. Patent
and Trademark Office and elsewhere.

If you would be interested in receiving protective vinyl
covers for your Loveswept books, please write to this address
for information:

Loveswept
Bantam Books
P.O. Box 985
Hicksville, NY 11802

ISBN 0-553-21853-0

Published simultaneously in the United States and Canada

Bantam Books are published by Bantam Books, Inc. Its trademark, consisting of the words "Bantam Books" and the por-
trayal of a rooster, is Registered in U.S. Patent and Trademark
Office and in other countries. Marca Registrada. Bantam
Books, Inc., 666 Fifth Avenue, New York, New York 10103.

PRINTED IN THE UNITED STATES OF AMERICA

O   0 9 8 7 6 5 4 3 2 1

For Carolyn Nichols

One

Cabe Malone stepped through the open framework of the doorway and walked to the center of the large room. He planted his hands on his hips and allowed his imagination full rein as he looked around.

He envisioned in his mind a roaring, welcoming blaze in the fireplace, with an overstuffed sofa and chairs grouped around it. The entire room would be filled with an aura of peace and contentment, beckoning to a man at the end of a hard day's work.

He scooped a handful of wood curls from the floor and smiled as he watched them sift through his fingers. He could smell the lingering aromas of dry wall and plaster as he walked slowly into the kitchen.

This was a good-sized room, he thought, and would still be as sunny and bright even after there was glass in the windows and curtains were hung. A family would gather here to share meals, and the sound of laughter would bounce off the ceiling.

He mentally placed shiny appliances against the bare walls and added a table and chairs. There would be a dog, too, he decided, scampering around right in the thick of things, waiting for someone to sneak him a scrap of food under the table.

He chuckled, and wandered back into the living room, stepping over a small pile of lumber. He shoved his hands into the back pockets of his jeans as he scrutinized the area, missing no detail of the workmanship.

Right on the money, he thought approvingly. Everything was done to perfection. This house, and the other five under construction on that section of land, were of the finest quality. They would stand sturdy and strong for generations to come.

He liked that feeling of continuity. No, he *needed* it, had to have it in his life just then. It gave him an anchor, a sense of security, to realize that this house and the others would still be there long after he was dead and gone. *He* controlled the destiny of this wood and plaster and brick. *He* decided that it had permanence, and no one could change that. People might come and go, but the house would remain, waiting to welcome the next family to walk through the front door.

He could hear the birds singing in the trees near the house. Soon the leaves would begin to turn to vibrant shades of orange, red, and yellow; splashes of color surrounding the yet-unadorned houses. He closed his eyes and inhaled deeply the aromas of wood, plaster, and sawdust. It was better than the most expensive perfume money could buy, he thought. This was real, earthy, created by hard, honest labor and craftsmanship. It touched his soul with a soothing hand. Yes, he really needed this.

And then he heard a sound. The sound of someone crying.

He opened his eyes and stiffened, straining his ears to determine where the sad sound was coming from. Someplace upstairs, he decided. He walked across the room and up the stairs. Treading softly, he made his way down a hall, following the sobs. He stopped at the door to one of the bedrooms and saw her.

She was sitting on the floor, her back against the wall. She'd drawn her knees up, hugging them with her arms, and her face was buried in her sleeve. She was crying as though her heart were breaking, and Cabe fought the urge to turn and bolt back down the stairs.

Instead his gaze flickered over her. The sunlight streaming in the window opening bathed her in a golden glow. It glinted on her wavy auburn hair, which fell in a tumbled disarray to her shoulders. Her slim-fitting jeans revealed the shapeliness of her slender legs, and her green sweater clung to her gently rounded breasts. With her face hidden he had no idea what she looked like or how old she was, but her figure told him she was a woman, not a child.

What in the hell should he do? Cabe asked himself. Leave her alone, granting her the privacy she'd obviously sought when she'd taken refuge in this half-finished house? But what if she was mentally unbalanced? What if she decided to leave through the window, instead of going down the stairs? He didn't need this hassle. He was the last person on earth equipped to give comfort to this grief-stricken woman. But he couldn't just walk away from her.

With a resigned shake of his head, he walked over to her and sat down on the floor. As he leaned his back against the wall and crossed his legs at the ankle, he saw her body tense. She made a funny little hiccup as she attempted to stop crying, but she didn't lift her head. She sat in the same pose, although now ramrod-stiff, as though frightened about what might happen next.

"Ever since I was a little boy," he said quietly, "my mother drummed it into my head that I should never, ever leave the house without a clean handkerchief in my pocket." He reached in his back pocket and took out a neatly folded handkerchief. "Now here I am, thirty-four years old, and still putting a handkerchief in my pocket every morning before I leave the house. It's taken all these years to realize my mother knew what she was talking about. I've finally found someone who needs my handkerchief."

Penelope Chapman lifted her head just enough to peer at the man sitting beside her. She blinked away her tears and focused on a pair of tattered tennis shoes. She shifted her head slowly, her gaze sweeping over long, muscular legs clad in faded jeans and across narrow hips and a flat stomach. She saw a large, tanned hand holding a white hankerchief toward her, and a tan T-shirt stretched across a broad chest and wide shoulders.

He had a face, of course, she thought, but she was too embarrassed to look at him. There she sat, trespassing and crying her eyes out. She had never done anything so humiliating in her life.

"Take the hankerchief," the man said gently.

Still peering at his chest over the top of her arm, she opened one hand. The man chuckled and placed the hankerchief in her palm.

He had a nice voice, she thought. So deep and rich and soothing. She really should look at his face, she supposed. And she really should thank him for the handkerchief, because her nose was running like a sieve, but she was absolutely mortified.

"So far," the man said, "I know you have great big brown eyes and very pretty slender fingers. I like your hair, too. It's all different shades when the sun is pouring over it like that."

He had to be kidding, Penelope thought incredulously. He liked her *hair?* It was a mess. And the way he'd said "great big brown eyes" made it sound as if she had the most fascinating eyes since Bambi. Her eyes were brown, simply brown. And they were probably red and swollen, too, from her crying jag. He certainly had a way with words, whoever he was. What did he look like, this man with the magnificent body and the voice like rich molasses? And what was his name?

"My name is Cabe."

She looked at his face . . . and stopped breathing.

She looked at the deep cleft in his chin, his high cheekbones, the sensual lips, the straight nose. His eyes were the bluest she had ever seen, and his thick, sun-streaked blond hair was badly in need of a trim. He was the most ruggedly handsome man she had ever seen in her twenty-seven years, and she wondered absently if she was going to pass out.

" 'Lo," she mumbled, then turned her head and

blew her nose. Now what? she wondered. He was watching her. She could feel his eyes on her. She had absolutely no idea what to do or what to say to this man, who was so masculine, so incredibly virile and earthy. She'd never been this close to a man like him before. He even smelled different from the men she knew, exuding aromas of soap and sweat and an undefinable scent that shouted male.

"Do you have a name?" he asked.

"No."

"Oh, okay," he said, laughing softly. "Your folks never got around to naming you, huh?"

She turned her head to look at him again. "I mean, yes, I have a name but . . . Yes, all right, it's Penel— It's Penny."

"Hello, Penny," he said. She was beautiful, he thought. Tearstained face, red nose with a dusting of freckles, and all, she was really lovely. And she was also very, very sad. "Want to talk about it?"

"About what?"

"Why you were crying."

"No. Thank you, but no." She dabbed at her nose with the handkerchief.

"Sometimes it helps to talk about what's ripping you up, but other times . . ." He shrugged. "Other times it doesn't do a damn bit of good. You just have to find a way to live with whatever it is."

"You sound as if you know about being sad," she said softly.

"I know."

She nodded, then leaned back against the wall. She let her legs slide down and stretch out in front of her. Staring straight ahead, she didn't speak.

Cabe didn't speak either. They sat there in the warm circle of sunshine, each lost in his own thoughts as the minutes ticked away.

When Cabe reached for her hand, she welcomed the warmth and strength of his touch. She didn't draw away when he pressed her hand flat on his hard thigh and covered it firmly with his own callused hand. It felt natural and right to have his hand on hers, to feel the heat of his leg beneath her palm. Penelope Chapman didn't do the things she was doing, but the minuscule part of her that was Penny did.

Still, she should retrieve her hand, she thought. She should get to her feet, politely thank Cabe for the use of his handkerchief, and march her little self right down those stairs and out the door. She should, but she wasn't going to, and she knew it. Nothing she had done so far today was remotely close to her normal behavior, so why start now? She just wanted to sit there in the sunshine next to this man, who was stroking her hand with his thumb and causing a funny fluttering in the pit of her stomach. Just sit there with Cabe.

She glanced at him from beneath her lashes. Her eyes immediately popped wide open as she discovered that he was watching her, a small smile tugging at the corners of his lips.

"Is something wrong?" she asked. Her voice was strangely breathless.

"Not at all. I was just looking at you."

"Why?"

"Because I like the way your hair changes color in

the sunlight. And because you seem like you're deciding if you should cut and run."

"Well, I—I've never trespassed before. I really shouldn't be here."

"It's Saturday. The construction crews won't be coming around."

"Why are *you* here?" she asked. She really should retrieve her hand. And she would. In a minute.

"I like to wander through these houses alone. It's . . . I don't know . . . peaceful. When we're all here working during the week it's noisy, hectic."

"You're a construction worker?" Lord, her mother would die, she thought. There sat her precious and proper darling with her hand on a construction worker's thigh!

Cabe hesitated. "Yeah, I'm a construction worker." Sort of, he rationalized to himself. Some of the time. When he wasn't busy supervising the ever-growing Malone Construction Company. When he wasn't tied up in meetings and putting together projects that would make a lot of money for a lot of people. When he couldn't stand to be cooped up inside for another minute, then he was a construction worker. "What do you do, Penny?"

"Penny," she repeated softly, staring at the handkerchief in her hand. "It sounds so strange hearing someone other than Aunt Beth call me that. To everyone else, I'm Penelope."

"Aunt Beth?"

She turned her head to look outside, blinking back the fresh tears that sprang to her eyes.

"Penny?" Cabe said, squeezing her hand.

"She died," Penelope said softly. "She was eighty-two years old, she'd lived a full life just the way she wanted to, and she was content, at peace. She was even rather excited about where she might find herself after death. I knew all that, but when I started sorting through her things this morning I—I just didn't want her to be gone. I wanted her to call me Penny, shoo me into a chair at the kitchen table, and fix me a baked apple with cinnamon and fresh cream. Her house always smelled like cinnamon. But not today. It was cold and so quiet. So very quiet."

Cabe touched her cheek and turned her head toward him. "I understand."

"I understand too," she said as two tears slid down her cheeks. "I understand that I'm being foolish and childish, and I'm not facing facts. Aunt Beth is dead, and I know that. Oh, Cabe, I ran. I'd changed into these clothes, which I'd left there ages ago, and started to look through Aunt Beth's things, and I suddenly couldn't stand it. I just ran out the door. I hardly remember coming into this house. I can't believe I behaved that way."

He frowned. "Why not?"

"Because I don't do things like this," she said almost angrily. She pulled her hand free from beneath his.

"You don't grieve for a loved one? You don't cry when you're sad?"

"No," she said, shaking her head. "I don't cry. Ever."

"Why not? There's nothing wrong with tears, Penny."

"I'm not Penny," she yelled. "I'm Penelope."

"You've totally lost me here," he said, shaking his head in confusion.

"Never mind," she said wearily. She leaned her head back against the wall and closed her eyes. "It's not important."

"I think it is," he said, his voice low. It is? he asked himself. This was nuts. Why should he care if she had hang-ups about her name, about crying, and Lord only knew what else? He had enough problems of his own. He should get up right now and get the hell out of there. And he had ten bucks that said he wasn't going to do it. Damn. "Penny—"

"Penelope," she interrupted, and sniffled into the handkerchief.

"No," he said, crossing his arms over his chest. "Penny. Penelope sounds stuffy, like somebody who sticks her nose in the air."

She laughed. She wasn't sure why she laughed, but since nothing else she had done so far that day had made much sense, she gave way to the laughter that bubbled up inside her.

Cabe made no attempt to hide his surprise; nor did he suppress his smile. What a great sound her laughter was, he thought. Her big, dark eyes were dancing, and she looked so beautiful, so young and carefree.

"Sorry," she said, gasping for breath. "It was just so funny, and so true! It is a stuffy, nose-in-the-air name." She paused, then added soberly, "And I'm a perfect Penelope."

His smile slowly faded as he studied her face. "No, I don't think you are. You're Penny. Your aunt Beth knew it, too."

"No, I . . ." She couldn't breathe when he looked at her like that! "I'm definitely a Penelope."

"Are you?" His voice was low and rumbly, and his head started to lower toward hers. "Are you really so very sure of that?"

Oh, good Lord, she thought frantically, he was going to kiss her. She had to stop him. She couldn't allow it. She didn't do things like this. Penelope Chapman didn't kiss construction workers in half-built houses. She . . . really . . . had . . . to stop him.

His intense gaze swept over her face as his beautiful mouth came closer and closer to hers, until she could feel his warm breath on her lips. A wondrous trembling swept through her, and she closed her eyes.

"Ah, Penny, I found you, Penny," he murmured, and feathered his lips over hers. "Are you"—his lips brushed hers again—"going to be"—and again—"my Lucky Penny?"

In the next instant he took full possession of her mouth, his tongue sliding with insistent pressure along her bottom lip. She hesitated only a moment, then parted her lips as her arms lifted to twine around his neck. His tongue met hers, and they dueled and danced together.

Never had there been such a kiss, Penelope thought hazily. It wasn't just a meeting of lips; it was a merging of senses. Her bones seemed to be melting from a liquid heat that flowed from deep within her, spreading throughout her. It was wonderful, and she never wanted it to end.

Malone! Cabe yelled at himself. Knock it off! He

had to stop kissing her, he really did. Penny was vulnerable in her grief for her aunt, and he was playing on those emotions, scum that he was. But she felt so good, and tasted so good, and—No! He had to stop.

He dragged his mouth from hers. "Penny," he said hoarsely.

"Yes?" she asked. Was that her voice? she wondered. That breathy little sound was *her* voice?

He cleared his throat. "I think that I should stop kissing you now, before things get out of control." Lord, what a corny thing to say.

She couldn't believe he'd actually said that, she thought, slowly opening her eyes. "What?"

With his hands on her shoulders he gently moved her away from him, then dragged a restless hand through his hair.

"You heard me," he said gruffly. "You don't strike me as the type who would have a quickie on a bare floor in a half-built house."

"Well!" she said, coming out of her rosy glow with a thud. "You don't have to be crude about it."

He smiled. "That got your attention."

"You've made your point," she said, sighing. "I haven't been behaving like myself all day. I certainly don't go around kissing the living daylights out of men I don't know. In fact, I don't kiss the socks off men I *do* know. Actually, this is rather frightening. It's like there're two of me, or something. You know, Penelope and Penny. Forget that. It's too ridiculous even to think about. Next thing I know, I'll be dashing off to see an analyst."

Cabe laughed. "Well, sure. Every yuppie worth his salt has an analyst."

"I haven't even figured out what a yuppie is."

"Don't worry about it. It's probably just a fad. The yuppies will fade out like the hippies did."

"I suppose. Well, I guess I should go back over to Aunt Beth's and get to work sorting her things. She left the house and everything in it to me. Aunt Beth never married. She was deeply in love once, when she was young, but it didn't work out. Never mind. You're not interested in all this. I really don't know what to do with the house. I hate to sell it, but it's a hundred-mile drive up here from Detroit. I could go months at a stretch and not have time to come for a quiet weekend. Why am I blithering on about all of this?"

"Because I'm listening," Cabe said quietly. "Because sometimes it helps just to say things out loud so you can get a clearer picture of them. Meadow View is more than miles away from Detroit, Penny. It's a world apart as far as tempo, pressure, and lifestyle go. Maybe you should hold on to the house for a while until you're certain you know what you want to do. It's none of my business, of course. I just thought I'd put in my two cents' worth."

"And I appreciate it," she said. "My parents assume I'm up here getting the house ready to be put on the market. They consider it a nuisance."

"But it's *your* house."

"Well, yes, but it isn't very practical to keep it."

"Do you always do what's practical?"

"Yes. But, don't count today. Today I'm weird."

"Nope. Today you're Penny. Today we shared kisses

that could start a brush fire. Today you cried and then laughed. I'm glad you picked this house to run to, Penny. I really am."

Their eyes met, and the now-familiar silence fell. The song of birds and the golden sunlight that poured onto them seemed to enclose them in their own world, and time lost meaning.

"Good Lord," Penelope muttered finally, pulling her gaze from his.

"Tell me about it," Cabe said. "You turn me inside out when you look at me like that."

"I'd better get back to Aunt Beth's." She stood up, and nearly cheered when she discovered her legs were going to support her. Cabe pushed himself up to stand beside her. "Oh, your handkerchief," she said. "If you'll give me your address, I'll mail it to you after I wash it."

"I'd rather you returned it in person," he said. "I want to see you again, Penny. How long are you staying in Meadow View?"

"I'm not sure," she said, looking up at him. Oh, those darned eyes of his, she thought. No one should have eyes that blue, eyes that could radiate so many different messages. It just wasn't fair. "I'll be here a few days, I guess."

"Plenty of time to get a handkerchief washed. Come on." He took her arm. "I'll give you a ride to your aunt Beth's house."

"I'll walk," she said, pulling her arm free.

"Penny, Penny." He frowned and shook his head. "You're starting to come across as a Penelope."

"I *am* a Penelope."

"Not in Meadow View," he said, flashing her a

dazzling smile. "It's not allowed. Your aunt Beth called you Penny here, and so do I. Being a Penelope in Mountain View simply isn't socially acceptable behavior."

She laughed. "You're crazy."

"And you," he said, trailing his thumb over her lips, "are beautiful when you laugh. Hell, you're beautiful when you're crying, but there's just something special about your laughter."

"Thank you, Cabe," she said softly. "That's a lovely thing to say."

"It's true." He really did like the sound of her laughter, he thought. It warmed him inside, in a place that was cold. Lord, he was getting corny again. What was it about this Penny that turned him into a cornball poet? "I'll give you a ride to Aunt Beth's house," he said quickly.

She smiled this time. "That would be nice."

He kissed her once more, a light but lingering kiss, then led her from the room. Downstairs in the living room, Penelope glanced around.

"This is going to be a marvelous room when it's finished," she said. "I can picture a huge fire in the fireplace and some overstuffed chairs gathered around it."

"And a family?"

"Oh, of course. This house is much too big for a single person. There should be three children, maybe four."

"And a dog."

"If you get a dog, then I get to have a kitten," she said, then glanced quickly at him when she realized what she'd said.

He nodded. "Sounds fair. A cat for you, a dog for me."

"Okay," she said, then hurried to the front doorway, hoping Cabe wouldn't notice the flush of embarrassment on her cheeks.

"Penny?" he said.

She turned. "Yes?"

"Do you realize we don't even know each other's last names?"

"Yes, I know. Can we just leave it like that? You'll be Cabe, and I'll be . . ." Her voice trailed off.

"Who? Who will you be?" he asked, moving to stand beside her.

Penelope lifted her chin and looked directly into his eyes.

"Here, in Meadow View . . ." She took a deep breath. "In Meadow View I'm Penny."

He circled her shoulders with his arm. "That, my Lucky Penny, is the best news I've had all day."

Two

Outside, Penny looked around at the area where the houses were being built.

"This is really very pretty," she said. "I didn't pay any attention when I came running in here. The houses are arranged so attractively, so each one has a good deal of land."

"Yep," Cabe said. "And a lot of trees. We don't just come in and plow everything under. Malone Construction believes in preserving the environment as much as possible."

"Your boss sounds like a man after my own heart."

He smiled. "That's good. Look, I might as well tell you that I'm—"

"Is that your truck?" she interrupted.

He followed the direction of her wide-eyed gaze, and laughed. "That's my pride and joy. It's a beauty, isn't it?"

"It's very—" she hesitated as she searched urgently

for an appropriate word, "interesting. Yes, that's the most interesting truck I've ever seen. I . . . um, think I'll walk back to Aunt Beth's, Cabe. The fresh air will do me good."

"Don't be silly." He sprinted to the truck and opened its creaking passenger door. "Madam," he said, with a sweeping gesture, "your chariot awaits."

Penny walked slowly to the truck, gazing in horror at it. It was wrinkled, she thought. The whole truck was wrinkled. There were only snatches of smooth metal, and at least six different colors of paint had been thrown on it in a hit-or-miss fashion. Most of it, though, a nondescript gray, and it looked like a wrinkled filing cabinet. She'd never been in a pickup truck in her life, let alone one like this!

"It won't bite," Cabe said, grinning at her. "Runs as smooth as glass."

"If you say so," she said, peering inside the cab as she pushed Cabe's handkerchief into her back pocket. "Bright-red upholstery? That's quite . . . cheerful, isn't it? Well, here I go, climbing in now." She didn't move. She heard Cabe's low, sexy chuckle behind her, and turned to glare at him. His expression was pure innocence.

"Need some help?" he asked, raising his eyebrows.

"No. Any dolt knows how to get into a truck." She lifted one foot inside, then hesitated. What was she supposed to grab onto? she wondered frantically. The open door was way over there, the dashboard was way over there, and the steering wheel was way the heck over there! This was ridiculous. And impossible!

Cabe cleared his throat.

She snapped her head around and glared at him again, then gasped as his large hands grasped her waist and he lifted her onto the seat.

"All set?" he asked, grinning.

"Certainly," she said, fluffing her hair with one hand. "I would have figured it out in a minute, you know."

"I'm sure you would have," he said solemnly, but she saw the merriment dancing in his blue eyes.

When he was settled in the driver's seat he turned the key in the ignition. The engine roared to life, and the entire truck started to shake.

"Great engine," he said, patting the dashboard. "I rebuilt it myself as a hobby. This truck is a classic."

"It's something, all right," Penny muttered, then yelled, "Oh, Lord!" as Cabe shifted gears and the vehicle shot forward. She gripped the dashboard with both hands.

"Where to?" he asked.

"The last house on Willow," she said, not relinquishing her hold. "Are you sure this thing is safe? It's going to shake itself to death."

"Shame on you. Don't you know there's an unwritten code that says you never, ever insult a man's truck? Them is fightin' words, ma'am."

"Sorry," she said. "This is the nicest truck I've ever ridden in."

"Oh, yeah?" He laughed. "Could it be that it's the *only* truck you've ever ridden in?"

"That's a technicality."

"Well, it's a good thing that you're Penny, and not Penelope. I can't see a Penelope appreciating this fine vehicle. Penny, that dashboard isn't going to fall off. You can let go of it."

"Oh, yes, of course," she said. She cautiously released her hold and moved back in the seat. Well, she thought, she liked the idea that Cabe was obviously a simple, down-to-earth man. Like the half-built house they'd been in, there was nothing fancy or phony about him. But this truck was taking the premise a tad too far. But then again, it wasn't so bad once a person got used to it. So what if the fillings in her teeth rattled loose? She could handle this. She hoped.

Cabe turned a corner, and with a yelp she was suddenly sliding across the seat, her arms and legs seeming to go in four different directions. Cabe flung out his arm and snagged her around the waist, hauling her close to his side.

"Hi, there," he said, dropping a quick kiss on her nose. He kept his arm tightly around her as he came to a stop sign.

"No wonder men like trucks," she said.

He smiled. "They have their uses. It's only featherweights who come flying across the seat, though."

"Well, if you'll let me go, I'll crawl back over to my side."

"Nope, you're safer right here. You might go sailing out the window next time. Quit wiggling around," he added as he reached over with his left hand to shift gears. "You're supposed to drape your arm around my neck and put your head on my shoulder. There're rules about this pickup stuff, you know."

This wasn't funny, Penny told herself firmly. It was absurd. Embarrassing and absurd. If her friends could see her now . . . No, it certainly wasn't one bit funny.

She burst into laughter.

With her arm draped around Cabe's neck and her head on his shoulder, she laughed until she could hardly breathe. And, oh, it felt good. The painful grief was being replaced by the warmth of her own laughter and the feel of Cabe's strong body; by the sensation of being young and not having a care in the world.

"There's that beautiful sound again," Cabe said.

She smiled and nestled closer to him. There was something to be said, she decided, for the rules regarding pickups. She'd never snuggled in any vehicle with any man in her life! When she became Penny, she didn't mess around.

"Last house on Willow," Cabe announced. He pulled into the driveway and turned off the ignition. "Nice place."

She slowly lifted her head and drew her arm away from his neck. "It's small," she said, "but very cozy. There's a fireplace in the living room, and two bedrooms upstairs. It certainly isn't fancy, but it's . . . I don't know . . . welcoming, warm."

"It takes people to add those ingredients," he said, opening the truck door. "If it's warm and welcoming, it's because your aunt Beth made it seem that way."

"Yes, I guess you're right." She started to move toward the other door, but he stopped her.

"Hold it," he said. "You're breaking pickup rules again. You always slide out the driver's side."

"Why?"

He got out of the truck and turned back toward her. "I'll show you why. Come on."

She wiggled across the seat, under the steering wheel, and swung her feet out of the truck. "Now what?"

"Now," he said, grasping her waist, "this."

He lifted her off of the seat and slid her slowly, sensually down his body as she clung to his shoulders.

Hooray for the rules! she thought giddily.

And then Cabe kissed her.

Who would believe it? she mused dreamily. Penelope Fitzsimmons Chapman was being kissed in a driveway, in broad daylight, next to a wrinkled pickup. Penelope Fitzsimmons Chapman was being kissed by a construction worker who wore tight jeans and needed a haircut. And it was ecstasy.

At last Cabe lifted his head. "I'm going to stop kissing you," he said, his voice husky, "in about five hours, give or take a day or two. Lord, Penny, you feel like heaven itself." He chuckled. "Kissing you is like eating potato chips. I can't stop after just one." His voice dropped an octave lower, and his smile faded. "I want more and more. I want you, Penny."

She could feel the color drain from her face. "Cabe . . ."

"Shh. You look scared to death. What I said doesn't call for a reply. I'll see you in."

"Well!" she said too loudly when they reached the front door. "Here we are. Thank you for the ride. Good-bye, Cabe." She extended her hand.

He looked at her hand, her face, then her hand

again. "What's this?" he asked, waving his hand over the top of hers.

"My hand," she said, frowning.

"I can see that . . . Pen-el-ope. If you think I'm going to shake your hand to say good-bye, you're nuts."

"Well, excuse me," she said with an indignant sniff. She spun around and opened the door.

"You left the door unlocked?"

"I was upset at the time. Good-bye." She marched inside, and he was right behind her. She turned to face him, planting her hands on her hips. "I don't recall inviting you in here."

"You invited the whole town in when you left the door unlocked." He glanced around and whistled. "Your aunt Beth was really into furniture, huh? I've never seen so much stuff in one room."

"I know," Penny said. "It's rather overwhelming. Aunt Beth was a collector. She couldn't bear to throw anything away. There are boxes in the basement, and every closet is full. I don't even know where to start."

"She left all this to you?" he asked, roaming around the room.

"Yes. You see, I'm the only one who got along with Aunt Beth. She was my mother's sister, but they were never close. Aunt Beth taught school in Detroit for thirty years, then retired here in Meadow View. She hadn't seen or spoken to the rest of the family in years. My parents let me visit her, but I'd come on the bus when I was still too young to drive. I adored her. I also used to think all this clutter was enchanting, but at the moment I'm not too thrilled. What am I going to do with all this stuff?"

Cabe picked up a figurine off an end table. "Maybe some of it's valuable. You know, priceless antiques or something."

"No, it isn't. Aunt Beth didn't believe in owning things because they were worth money. She never approved of my parents' emphasis on material possessions. Aunt Beth kept all these things simply because she liked them and they gave her pleasure."

"There's nothing wrong with that," Cabe said, setting the figurine back in place. "A person could get claustrophobia in here, though. There's hardly room to move around."

"The whole house is like this. Aunt Beth was a compulsive cleaner, too. There was never a speck of dust anywhere."

He laughed. "There wasn't room for a speck of dust."

"You're probably right," Penny said, smiling.

"Why did you get so up-tight out by the truck when I said I wanted you?"

"Pardon me?" she said, startled by the sudden change of topic.

"You heard me. You knew I wanted you, from the way I was kissing you at the construction site. Why did it throw you for a loop when I said it outside?"

"Well . . ." she stared at the toe of her shoe. "Because—because that other house almost seemed to be in another world. But here, I was standing in Aunt Beth's driveway and—"

"And because you wanted me too?"

Her head snapped up. "I never said that."

"Yes, you did." He walked slowly toward her. "You said it with your eyes"—she began to back up—"and with your lips and tongue." He continued advancing toward her, and she thudded against the door. "You said it with your body when you molded it to mine." He stopped in front of her and braced his hands on the door on either side of her head, keeping his body away from hers. She stared up at him with wide eyes, her heart racing. "Oh, yes, Penny, you told me that you wanted me."

"No," she whispered.

"And now?" he murmured, lowering his head toward hers. "What about now? Do you still want me, Penny?"

"No. Stop it. Why are you doing this?"

"I don't know." His lips brushed against hers and, despite herself, she sighed. "All I know is that I have an ache in my gut for you. You've cast some kind of weird spell over me, Penny. I've never desired a woman the way I do you. I want you *now*, and I can't have you, because you're sad and vulnerable, and you'd probably hate me afterward. I'm not used to being tied up in knots, and I think nobility stinks." He paused. "Oh, hell. Forget it."

"Cabe—"

"Quiet," he said gruffly, then took possession of her mouth in a hard, searing kiss.

The punishing kiss sent a flash of panic through Penny, and she pressed her hands flat on Cabe's chest in a futile attempt to push him away. In the next instant the kiss gentled, and, seemingly of their own volition, her hands inched upward to encircle his neck and tangle in his thick hair. Shock waves of desire rocketed through her as his tongue met hers, and her knees trembled when she heard a groan rumble up from his chest.

He moved closer to her, then closer yet, until his body pressed hers against the door and her breasts were crushed to his chest in a sweet pain. The heat from his firm body surrounded her, igniting her passion further. He shifted his hands to cup her head, his mouth continuing its frenzied onslaught. She could feel his arousal hard against her.

She was living in stolen moments, she thought hazily. She was Penny, not Penelope. She was a woman who wore jeans and allowed her hair to fall free about her shoulders. A woman who knew how to cry and how to laugh. She rode in a pickup and trespassed to seek solace in a half-built house. And in her stolen moments, in her stolen place, she had found a man like none she'd ever known before. A man who wasn't polished, refined, or genteel, but who was earthy and real, rough-edged and honest.

And she wanted him.

It was all separate and apart from Penelope Fitzsimmons Chapman. This world, this man, this want and need, were Penny's.

A moan escaped from her throat as she arched into his strong body. The passionate sound slammed against Cabe's brain, pulling him slowly back from the raw need raging in him. With restraint that caused his muscles to tremble, he tore his mouth from hers.

"Lord, what am I doing?" he muttered, not realizing he'd spoken out loud.

"Kissing me," Penny whispered. "Holding me and

kissing me. Oh, Cabe, I do want you. You were right, and I admit it."

He looked at her moist, kiss-swollen lips, at the flush of passion on her cheeks and the smoky hue of desire reflected in her big, dark eyes. He filled his senses with the feel of her soft body pressed to his, with her sweet, feminine aroma. He gritted his teeth against the aching coil of need twisting within him, and with what seemed like his last ounce of self-control, he pulled her hands from his neck and stepped back.

"No," he said.

No, she repeated dully. No? He was rejecting her? Now? After creating a fire within her, a raging, burning fire of need and want, he was stepping away? Why?

"Why?"

"I told you why," he said, raking a hand through his hair. "This isn't the time."

"Because you say it isn't," she said, her voice rising as anger pushed aside her desire. "I was under the impression that this type of thing should be decided by mutual consent. I'm not the vulnerable, weepy mess you seem to think I am. I'm a woman, and I want you."

Cabe shoved his hands into his back pockets and stared up at the ceiling for a long moment. When he looked at her again, she could see a muscle jumping along his tightly clenched jaw and his pulse beating wildly at the base of his throat.

"You don't understand," he said gruffly.

"Then explain it to me. Tell me why you're rejecting me. I think I deserve to know."

His hands shot out, and he gripped her by the shoulders. "Rejecting you? Is that what you think is going on here?"

"Yes."

"Dammit, Penny, I'm trying to keep from using you! I was telling myself you were too upset over your aunt Beth to handle our making love, but that was a lie. I saw the change in you after you'd cried, saw you find an inner peace about your aunt's death. I knew you were going to be all right."

"And? So?"

"*I* don't have that inner peace, Penny. I have so much churning inside of me there's hardly room for a breath of air. I can push it all away for a while by getting blind drunk or by having sex with an unimportant woman. You deserve better than that. I won't do it. I won't use you to quiet my demons. You're too special, Penny. Just too damn special."

Gazing up at him, Penny saw the pain deep in his blue eyes and etched in the hard set of his features. In the next instant, though, it was gone, as he seemed to gather his emotions and retreat into himself, creating a nearly palpable wall between them.

"I'd better go," he said quietly.

"I'd listen, you know, if you wanted to talk about what's troubling you," she said softly. "You were there for me when I needed you. That's what friends are for."

"Friends?" His laugh sounded brittle. "That isn't quite what I had in mind for us, Penny. I pictured us as lovers, not friends."

"Don't you think that your lover should also be

your friend? Someone you can trust and believe in, someone you know will be there for you?"

"No," he said, shaking his head. "Friendship doesn't have to play a part in what two people share in bed. Look, I'll get out of your way and let you get started sorting through this stuff. Penny, I'm sorry if I upset you in any way. That wasn't my intention."

"You didn't upset me. I'm very glad you found me in that house, Cabe."

"I found my Lucky Penny." He brushed his lips lightly over hers, then reached behind her to open the door. She stepped out of the way. "See you later, okay?" he said, turning to look at her.

"Yes."

He gazed at her for a long, heart-stopping moment, then left the house and closed the door quietly behind him. Penny didn't move. She stood perfectly still until the sound of his truck faded away in the distance. Then she drew a shaky breath and rested her fingers lightly on her lips.

Cabe was a very complicated man, she realized, sinking onto the nearest chair. He was fun and warm, tender and sensitive, and yet very troubled. What were these demons that stalked him, that put that pain in his eyes? What had happened to him?

She sighed. Now what? she wondered, getting to her feet. Would he come back while she was still in Meadow View? Would she open the door and find him standing there smiling at her? Probably not. She wasn't his type. He wanted sexual release, pure and simple. He wanted a woman who played that game. He wanted to escape for a while to a place where his demons couldn't follow him. He didn't even want a friend.

"Oh, Cabe," she said, picking up a throw pillow and hugging it to her breasts, "thank you for today. Thank you for giving me a chance to be Penny for some stolen moments."

She sighed again; then, with dragging steps, went in search of some empty boxes.

Cabe pulled into the driveway of a large two-story house and turned off the ignition. He folded his arms on the top of the steering wheel and stared at the house and the trees surrounding it. Memories of his youth assaulted him as his gaze lingered on the tree he'd tumbled from when he'd been eight years old, resulting in a broken arm. Jason had been so jealous of his cast, their mother had finally wrapped Jason's arm in gauze, which had satisfied the little boy.

At the thought of Jason, the familiar chill, the pain and the anger, filled him again. Cabe and Jason, Jase and Cabe, always together, full of the devil, and seeming never to run out of energy. They'd grown up in this house, fought, laughed, and loved here. Cabe and Jase, the Malone twins, double trouble, always on the move.

And now Jason was dead.

He was six months buried in the ground, and the hurt was still an open wound within Cabe, as if Jason had died only yesterday. The pain was raw because it never had a chance to diminish. Every time he walked into that house, he was forced to face the truth.

The wrong brother had died.

Cabe was pulled from his tormented thoughts as the front door of the house burst open and a little girl ran out. He smiled and slid out of the truck, extending his arms to her as she barreled forward, flinging herself at him. She squealed in delight as he lifted her high above his head. Looking up at her, he saw a mirror image of himself at her age—the big blue eyes, the blond hair, the recognizable Malone features.

"Hello, pretty girl," he said, setting her on her feet.

"Hi. Grandma heard the truck and said if you want lunch you best get the lead out."

"That a fact?" Cabe said, chuckling. "Guess I'd better get the lead out, then. I swear, Holly Malone, you're prettier than when I left the house this morning. You didn't get married while I was gone, did you?"

"No," she said, and giggled behind her hand. "I'm only six years old."

"Oh, that's right," he said, snapping his fingers. "Guess you'll be around a while yet. You ought to wait until you're at least seven before you get married."

"You're silly, silly, silly," she said, laughing. "Oh, look. There's an airplane way up there in the sky."

"Yep."

"Do you think he's flying close to heaven, Uncle Cabe? Do you think my mommy and daddy can see that plane from where they are in heaven?"

"I don't know," Cabe said, feeling his throat tighten.

"I'm sorry, Holly, but I really don't know the answer to that."

"That's okay." She shrugged. "I'll ask Grandma. Where did you go this morning, Uncle Cabe?"

"Just over to look at those houses I'm building."

"Grandma said that was where she thought you'd gone, and she said you're working too hard."

"I wasn't working; I was just looking around. I found . . . I found a Lucky Penny."

"Really? Are you going to keep it forever? You're supposed to do that, you know, when you find a lucky penny. You're supposed to keep it forever and ever and ever. Are you gonna?"

"We'll see." He took her hand. "Let's go have some of this lunch I've been hearing about." Forever and ever and ever, he mused. Holly, in her little-girl world, didn't realize that there were no guarantees about anything, especially the tomorrows. She'd lost her parents, Jason and Karen, and still she believed in forevers. Incredible.

"Best wash your hands, Uncle Cabe," Holly said as they walked into the house.

"What? Oh, yeah, I'm going. Tell Grandma I'll be right there."

" 'Kay. I can skip. Watch me skip," she said, going off down the hall.

"You're the best skipper in Meadow View," he called after her, then went into the bathroom off the entry-way. He turned on the water in the sink and frowned at his reflection in the mirror. "Well, idiot?" he said. "Why did you leave Penny?" Why had he walked away from her when she'd looked at him with desire in her big brown eyes? Who was he kidding? He knew why. What blew his mind was that he had told her so many of his deepest feelings. There he'd stood in her living room, telling her she deserved better than a man consumed by demons. Damn, why had he revealed so much of himself? He'd always kept his feelings private, inside himself, where they belonged.

With a disgusted shake of his head he dried his hands, then walked down the long hall to the large, sunny kitchen at the back of the house.

"Food!" he bellowed. "I need food, or I'll gobble up a little girl with blond hair and blue eyes." Holly laughed in delight.

Martha Malone, an attractive woman in her fifties, turned from the stove. "What you need," she said to her son, "is a haircut."

"Naw," Cabe said, sitting down at the table. "Holly and I are having a contest to see who can grow the longest hair. Right, squirt?"

"Guess so," Holly said, shrugging. "Know what, Grandma? Uncle Cabe found a lucky penny. Can I see it, Uncle Cabe?"

"Oh, well, I have it in a special place. I hid it so no one else can have it." Now, that was an interesting thought. No one would touch Penny but him. No one would kiss or hold or caress or make love to Penny but him. Dammit, though, what about Penelope? How many men were waiting for Penelope in Detroit? "Damn," he muttered.

"Cabe, don't swear in front of Holly," Martha said.

"Sorry. Erase that word, Holly."

"My daddy used to say damn," Holly said, "but he said I couldn't say it until I was a hundred eighty-ninety years old, or something like that."

"And don't you forget it," Cabe said, tweaking her nose.

The kitchen door was pushed open and a plump, gray-haired woman in her sixties entered, carrying a tray.

Cabe lay his hand against his chest. "Be still, my heart," he said, rolling his eyes. "The love of my life just came into the room."

"Pshaw with your blarney, now," the woman said, with a heavy brogue. "In all my years of nursin', I've never met the likes of you, Cabe Malone. You've kissed the blarney stone for sure, you have."

"You wound me, lass," he said. " 'Tis true that you do."

"Cabe, hush," Martha said, smiling. "Tillie, how did Mr. Malone like his lunch?"

"He's a bit off his feed today," Tillie said. "I'll be takin' his custard back to him after his nap. He's a mite tired now, not thinkin' real clear, but we've all seen him on days like this, when he just can't be keepin' all his facts straight. He heard that clankin' old truck pull in and—"

"Thought it was Jase," Cabe said quietly.

"That he did," Tillie said, sighing. "I'm thinkin' he'll be better after his nap."

"You know he gets terribly confused since his stroke, Cabe," Martha said.

"Yeah," Cabe said. "Are we going to eat?"

Holly tugged on his sleeve. "Uncle Cabe?"

"Yeah, babe?" He smiled at her.

"I know you get sad when Grandpa forgets that my daddy is in heaven and thinks you're my daddy, then gets mad at you 'cause you're not. But maybe, now that you found your lucky penny, things will get better and Grandpa will like you just for being you."

"I—" Cabe started to reply.

"I think that sounds wonderful," his mother said, giving him a hard stare. "Don't you, Cabe?"

"Yeah, just great," he said. "Don't worry, Holly, everything is going to be fine." Just super, he thought dryly. It would take more than his Lucky Penny to change his father's attitude. The stroke hadn't altered Matthew Malone's feelings toward his black sheep of a son. Cabe was the outsider, the misfit, the nonconformist. Cabe was the thorn in Matthew's side.

And just hours before his stroke, on the day of Jason and Karen's funeral, Matthew had told Cabe that the wrong son had died.

Three

Cabe spent the afternoon painting the playhouse he had built for Holly in the backyard. The fact that she helped him caused the project to take twice as long as necessary, but he enjoyed her nonstop chatter and little-girl enthusiasm.

Despite Holly's presence, though, he often found his thoughts turning to Penny. She was, he decided, a fascinating woman. Her insistence that she was indeed a Penelope told him volumes. He knew he was glimpsing a part of her that very few people saw. He was seeing Penny, and he thought she was enchanting. She was open and honest, and felt like an angel in his arms.

But she hadn't really been in *his* arms, he thought as he cleaned up the paint supplies after he and Holly were through and the little girl had run back inside the house. Penny hadn't kissed Cabe, the owner of a highly successful construction company.

She hadn't kissed Cabe, the black sheep, the son who had never measured up in his father's eyes. She hadn't laughed and cried with the Cabe who was so filled with his own grief and confusion at the loss of his brother that his insides were twisted into painful knots.

No, she had been with Cabe, the construction worker, who made his living by back-breaking labor and drove a truck that appeared about ready to fall apart. Cabe, who needed a haircut, and wore faded jeans and grungy tennis shoes.

How strange, he mused as he sat down on the back-porch steps. Neither he nor Penny had presented an external self honestly in that half-built house this morning. Yet, despite that, he felt as though he'd known her forever. She *was* his Lucky Penny, and he'd been subconsciously searching for her for years.

Penny claimed she was Penelope, a prim and proper Penelope, who didn't cry or wear blue jeans. Yet somehow he knew that the woman he'd been with today was the real woman. Just as he had lowered the walls around him when he'd told her of his inner demons, so she had stripped away the phony facade and given him glimpses of the vulnerable person within. The desire that had throbbed hot and heavy through his aching body hadn't been just basic lust, as with the many women he'd known in the past. No, it had been desire, a desire to give her pleasure, to share with her the ecstasy of lovemaking. The entire situation was nuts, but it felt so damn right.

"Strange," he muttered, shaking his head.

"You're talking to yourself now?" his mother asked, stepping out onto the porch. "I suppose I shouldn't worry unless you start answering, or so they say. May I join you?"

"You bet," he said, patting the spot next to him. "Pull up a step and sit. I hope I got all of the paint off Holly. She got more on herself than on the playhouse."

"I gave her a bath to take care of the turpentine smell. She's having a snack with Tillie now. The playhouse is darling, Cabe. Holly is so excited about it. It was very good of you to build it for her."

"I love her, Mom. You know that."

"Yes, I know you do. Cabe, I want to talk to you."

"About?"

"You, your life, your future plans."

"All that?" he said, smiling at her. "And here I thought you were just going to nag me again about getting a haircut."

"Don't give me one of your dazzling smiles, young man. They don't work on me like they do on the rest of the female populace."

"Can't blame a guy for trying," he said with a shrug. "Okay, lay it on me. Me, my life, my future plans. What about them?"

"That's what I'm asking you. You have a large company to run in Detroit, and it must be suffering from your absence."

"I have competent people working for me."

"But you like to be on top of things, and you're not. Cabe, it's been six months since Karen and Jason were killed in that automobile accident, and six months since your father's stroke. You bought that parcel of land, custom-designed those homes, and now you're working as one of the crew to build them."

"So?"

"Cabe, I was grateful that you stayed on here after everything happened. I was so devastated, and I don't know what I would have done without you. We both know that your father isn't going to improve. He's paralyzed on the left side, and his mind isn't always clear. He'll never be the man he was. I've accepted that. Tillie is wonderful with him, and I know he's getting the best of care here, in his home, where he'd want to be. Holly is doing fine in school, and the counselor said her healing process over the loss of her parents is healthy and normal."

"I know all that. What's the bottom line that you're leading up to, Mom?" Cabe asked, peering at a blob of paint on his tennis shoe.

Martha took a deep breath, then lifted her chin. "You don't belong here anymore, Cabe."

He tensed, and anger was flashing in his eyes as he looked up at his mother. "What in the hell is that supposed to mean?"

"Just what I said. You're not living; you're existing. Cabe, listen to me. You know that I was there in the study the day of the funeral, that I heard the horrible thing your father said to you. But, Cabe, he was heartbroken over losing Jason and Karen. He didn't really mean what he said; he just lashed out at the first convenient person. He didn't honestly wish it had been you who had died instead of Jason."

"Yes, he did," Cabe said quietly. "Dad never forgave me for not joining the law firm. You know that.

He named it Malone and Sons the day Jason and I were born. But the rotten son refused to jump through the hoop. Oh, yeah, he meant what he said. He was mad as hell that I was standing there and his good boy, the son he was proud of, was dead."

"Oh, Cabe."

"I loved Jase. I never resented the place he had in our father's life, because I didn't want to be there. Jase was perfectly content to follow in Dad's footsteps. I just couldn't do it, but it didn't diminish what Jason and I had together. I'm not hanging around here waiting for Dad to figure out that I'm not such a bad guy. It just isn't going to happen."

"Why *are* you here, Cabe?"

"How can you ask me that? Holly is mine. Karen and Jason made me her guardian. She's my responsibility. What do you want me to do? Go back to Detroit and leave you with a six-year-old child to raise, on top of everything else you're dealing with?"

"I want you to get on with your life," Martha said, placing her hand on his forearm. "Cabe, you're playing mind games. I have Tillie, a cleaning lady, a gardener, all the help I need. Holly is a joy to me, not a burden. You have the right to take her to Detroit if you so choose, but you know she's happy here. Face it, Cabe, you're staying out of a misplaced sense of guilt over the fact that you're alive and Jason is dead."

"Hell," he muttered, getting to his feet. "That's ridiculous."

"Is it?" she said softly. "You're my son. I know you as well as I know myself. I see the pain in your eyes, the restlessness inside you. You can't go on like this. You have no debt to pay here, Cabe. It's time for you to go back where you belong."

Cabe walked several feet away and stood with his back to his mother, his hands curled into tight fists at his sides.

"I've made you angry," Martha said as she stood. "I expected that, but these things needed to be said. I love you, Cabe. I know you suffered when your father wouldn't accept your career choice, and I'm very sorry. I can't change any of the past, but I can urge you, beg you, to look to the future. Life is for those who are alive. It's as simple as that. Jason is dead. You can't even any scores, make things different, by ceasing to live the way you want to live. Please, Cabe, think about what I've said." She paused. "I'll leave you alone now."

Cabe didn't speak or move. He clenched his jaw so tightly that his teeth ached. Every muscle in his body was aching with tension. He heard the door close and knew his mother had gone back inside the house, but still he didn't move. Her softly spoken words reverberated inside his brain, and he drew a trembling hand down his face, willing himself to relax.

"Dammit, Jason," he said, his voice raspy as he stared up at the heavens. "You really screwed things up by getting yourself killed, do you know that? Hell, Jase. What am I going to do?"

He turned and strode from the yard, his steps heavy. A minute later he roared the battered truck into action and drove away from the house with a squeal of tires.

• • •

Around seven that evening Penny took a bath, then pulled on a full-length kelly green velour robe that zipped up the front. After donning a pair of bright red knee socks, she went downstairs and sank onto the sofa in front of the warm, welcoming fire she'd built.

She was exhausted, she realized, and for good reason. She'd accomplished a great deal that afternoon. She had packed Aunt Beth's clothes, a multitude of knickknacks, and odd dishes, and had found a thrift shop, which gave its proceeds to the needy, to come pick up the numerous cartons. It was just a dent in all that needed to be done, but it was a definite start in the right direction.

And while she'd worked, she'd thought of Cabe.

Penny sighed. As tired as she was, she was filled with a strange energy that left her edgy. If she didn't unwind, she mused, she'd never be able to sleep that night. There was nothing she wished to watch on television and she was too jumpy to concentrate on reading a book. What a way to spend a Saturday night.

If she were in Detroit she'd be going out with Tom, a young and already highly successful lawyer, to dinner and a play that had just opened. She'd had to cancel the date when Aunt Beth died, and had done so without regrets. The evening would have been like so many other ones—elegant and sedate—and Tom was like all the other men who took her out—bright, ambitious, financially well off, and in awe of her family. And, she'd been realizing lately, deathly boring.

What, she wondered, did a man like Cabe do on a

Saturday night? Shoot pool? Play poker with the boys? Oh, ha. Cabe's Saturday-night plans would most definitely include a woman. A sexy woman. A sexy, experienced, worldly woman. Would they end up in his bed or hers?

"Shame on you, Penelope Chapman," she said out loud. "That's none of your business."

Still her mind taunted her with visions of Cabe in bed. Beautiful Cabe naked, his tanned skin appearing even darker against cool white sheets. He'd smile that sexy smile of his, then move that powerful body over her and—

"Oh, Lord," she said as desire swirled within her. She pressed her hands to her flushed cheeks.

The Penny part of her was so naughty, she thought. She couldn't remember ever imagining one of Penelope's escorts nude! There were flesh-and-blood men beneath those perfectly tailored suits, but she'd never really dwelled on the subject. The men she dated were polite, practiced all the social graces, and kissed her good night with gentlemanly restraint. They smelled of expensive cologne and rich brandy, and while they might perspire during a game of racquet ball at the country club, she doubted if there was one among them who knew how to get down-and-dirty and actually sweat!

"Boring," she mumbled. None of them was Cabe. None had eyes as blue, shoulders as wide, a body so tightly muscled from hard labor. None evoked such powerful, overwhelming sensations within her, making her so incredibly glad she was a woman. There was only one Cabe, and the knowledge that she would never see him again was enough to bring on a black depression. "You would have liked him, Aunt Beth," she said, gazing into the fire.

Then she shifted her attention to the mantel, where Cabe's handkerchief lay, freshly washed and neatly ironed. Aunt Beth would tell her to use the handkerchief as a reason to go to the construction site on Monday to see Cabe. And Aunt Beth would urge her to find out the man's last name, for heaven's sake.

But no, Penny thought gloomily, there was no point. She'd wrap the handkerchief in tissue, put Cabe's name on it, and take it to the half-built house tomorrow while no one was there. Cabe would find it on Monday, and that would be that. She really didn't want to know his last name. They were simply Penny and Cabe, who had shared stolen moments that were now over.

But oh, such memories she now had.

How was it possible, she mused, that such a short period of time spent with Cabe could have such a tremendous effect on her? Why was it that by merely closing her eyes she could envision him so clearly, it was as though he were really there? How could it be that by remembering his touch she could feel desire once more rising within her? She didn't know. What she did know was that because Cabe had found her in that half-built house, she was never going to be the same again.

A knock sounded at the door, jarring her from her reverie. She got to her feet, fully expecting this to be another one of the neighbors wishing to express condolences. She really wasn't in the mood for any more of this, but it couldn't be helped. She plastered a pleasant expression on her face and opened the door.

It was Cabe.

No, it wasn't, she told herself firmly. It wasn't Cabe standing there on the porch. She was only imagining that he was there, because she'd been thinking about him.

"Hello, Penny."

"Cabe? Oh, heavens, it *is* you."

He shoved his hands into his pockets and hunched his shoulders against a chill wind that whipped around him.

"Am I disturbing you?" he asked. His gaze swept over her. "Were you headed for bed? I love the socks," he added, smiling.

"What?" She shook her head as if to clear it. "Oh, no, you're not disturbing me at all. I was just . . . Cabe, you must be freezing. Where's your jacket?"

"I came away without it. I've been out for a drive and lost track of the time . . . and the temperature, I guess."

"Well, come in by the fire."

"I thought you'd never ask," he said, and stepped inside the house.

Penny closed the door and leaned against it for a moment to catch her breath and to tell her knees to stop trembling. Cabe was here, she thought, right in front of her. It didn't seem real, somehow, because she'd been thinking about him, then up he popped and . . . Lord, she was acting like a ninny.

"Please, sit down," she said. "Would you like a cup of coffee to warm you up?"

"If it's no trouble."

"Not at all. Just weave your way through the obstacle course. I'll be right back."

"Green robe and red socks," he said, his gaze sliding slowly over her again. "You look like a Christmas present." He stared at the zipper tab. "Waiting to be opened."

Surprise! Penny thought wildly. There was nothing beneath the red-and-green wrapping but a nude body. Oh, good Lord, she didn't have a stitch on under her robe. Did Cabe know that? No, of course not. He wasn't Superman, with x-ray vision. She could be wearing a granny gown or flannel jammies, for all he knew. But if he kept looking at the zipper like that, he was going to melt it!

"I'll get the coffee," she said, and nearly walked into a floor lamp. "Excuse me," she said to it. "Go sit by the fire, Cabe. Okay? Okay. 'Bye."

Cabe smiled while Penny skirted around a rocking chair and an old-fashioned spinning wheel as she left the room. Cautiously he made his way to the sofa, stepping over a coffee table to get there.

Penny was shaken up, he realized as he sank onto the sofa with a weary sigh. She obviously hadn't been expecting him to appear at her front door. Truth of the matter was, *he* hadn't expected to appear there either. After driving for hours and rehashing everything that his mother had said, until he'd thought he'd blow a fuse in his brain, he'd just suddenly found himself at the last house on Willow, at Penny's.

He slouched down on the sofa, wiggling his feet under the coffee table, and laced his fingers on his chest. Resting his head on the back of the sofa, he stared into the nearly hypnotizing flames of the fire.

Penny looked awfully good in that robe, he thought. He supposed it was a Penelope robe, but the socks . . . Now, those red socks were one hundred percent Penny. She did look like a Christmas present just waiting to be unwrapped. Well, unzipped actually. And twenty bucks, *a hundred bucks*, said she had nothing on underneath but her funny red socks.

He shifted slightly as his body tightened at the image of Penny he was creating in his mind. Knock it off, Malone, he told himself. He hadn't come here to seduce Penny. Had he? No, of course not. But why in the hell was he here?

"Why are you here?" Penny asked.

"What?" Cabe jerked upward and whacked his shin on the coffee table. "Ow. Damn. This place is dangerous."

Penny set a tray containing two mugs, sugar, cream, and a plate of cookies on the coffee table, then sat down beside him.

"I'm sorry," she said. "My asking you why you're here is very rude."

"No, it isn't." He handed one of the mugs to Penny, then settled back with his own. "It's a legitimate, reasonable question. Thing is, I don't know the answer."

"You don't know why you're here?" she asked. "Have you been drinking?"

He chuckled. "No. Why does Penelope own crazy red socks?"

"She doesn't. I found them among the clothes I left here ages ago."

"Oh, so those *are* Penny's socks. That's what I thought."

"Actually, Cabe," she said, frowning, "this is getting rather weird. You know, speaking of Penelope and Penny as though they're—I'm—two separate people."

"No, it's not weird," he said, looking directly at her. "It's incredibly honest."

"What do you mean?"

"Think about it. A man and woman meet in some kind of social setting. A bar, a party, whatever. They play verbal games for a while, check each other out. They chat about the usual garbage—movies they've seen, books they've read, what they do for a living. Then they push a bit more, dig a little deeper to try to discover values, outlooks, opinions. They're both holding back a lot of personal things, because, after all, they really don't know each other, but they're keeping score, deciding whether to advance further or get the hell out. Are you following me?"

"Yes," she said, nodding.

"It wasn't like that with us, Penny. We didn't follow the rules of the dating game. We skipped over the phony stuff. There wasn't time to be cautious or clever, because everything was up-front, honest. We were Penny and Cabe, with no last names, no protective walls standing between us, nothing. No, this isn't weird; it's rare and special. I've said things to you that I won't admit to my own mother."

"The demons," she said softly. "The ones inside you that are haunting you."

"Yeah," he said gruffly, and took a swallow of coffee. He set his mug on the tray, then shifted to face her. "I couldn't get you off my mind after I left here today. I guess it's because of the way we met, what we shared, but I feel as though I've known you for a very long time. I feel as though I could say anything and everything to you, and you'd understand. You can tell me a hundred times that you're Penelope, but I wouldn't believe it. You're Penny. You were Penny when I found you, and you didn't have a chance to slip on a phony facade. You're my Lucky Penny, and nothing is going to convince me other-wise."

Penny set her mug down and stared into the fire. "I thought about you, too, Cabe," she said quietly. "I thought about how good it had felt to laugh with you and cry with you, to be Penny with you. We shared stolen moments, and I'll cherish them."

"They're not over. *We're* not over. Didn't you hear me, Penny? There's something very special happening between us. Are you just going to ignore it, walk away from whatever this might be?"

"It's not real!" she said, turning to face him.

"Dammit." He grasped her shoulders. "Yes, it is. That's what's so beautiful about what we're sharing, don't you see? You cried with me and laughed with me. I told you about the demons inside me. We reacted to each other from our guts, or our hearts, or however you want to say it. Nothing like this has ever happened to me before. Hell, I even thought about what you said about a lover being a friend, and it started to make sense! Penny, my life is so screwed up, but when I'm with you I feel free. Free to be me. Just Cabe. Just Cabe and his Lucky Penny."

"Oh, Cabe," she whispered, tears misting her eyes,

"I understand. There is no Penelope when I'm with you. I'm Penny, and oh, dear heaven, it feels so good. But—"

"No," he interrupted, lifting his hands to cradle her face. "Don't start looking for all the reasons why there's something wrong with this. It isn't wrong, Penny. We came together with such honesty and openness. Some people are in relationships for years and never have what we do now. Give us a chance, Penny. Don't throw all this, us, away." He brushed his lips over hers. "Don't do it to us, Penny. Please."

He kissed her. He kissed her so gently, so reverently, that a sob caught in Penny's throat. Her eyes drifted closed, and she clutched his shoulders for support. He kissed her cheeks, the freckles dusting her nose, then returned to her mouth. His tongue flicked over her lips, and a shiver of desire rippled through her.

"Oh, Cabe, please kiss me," she whispered. "Really kiss me."

Groaning, he gathered her close and took possession of her mouth, his tongue delving deep inside to meet hers. He shifted his legs, and without breaking the searing kiss, eased her back on to the sofa, stretching out on top of her. One hand slid down her side, loving the feel of the rich fabric of her robe, but wanting to touch her soft skin.

"Lord, you feel good," he said, his voice husky. "And taste good, and smell good." He pressed his hips firmly on hers, his arousal full and strong against her. "Can you feel that? Can you feel what you do to me, how much I want you?"

"Yes."

"Don't be afraid of me, Penny, not ever. We're not going to make love until you're very sure you're ready to take that step with me. I'm not going to do anything to frighten you away. Oh, Penny, your eyes are incredible. So big and dark, and they tell me so much. You're beautiful, my Lucky Penny. You truly are."

He claimed her mouth again, and Penny was lost in a sea of raging sensations. With her arms around him she drew him closer, needing to feel his heat, the power in his massive body. His manhood surged against her, and she lifted her hips to cradle him, to rejoice once more in her own femininity. There was nothing of importance beyond this man and what they would share as one.

Even in the hazy, passion-laden recesses of her mind, she realized she was filled with the greatest sense of peacefulness she had ever known. While her body hummed with sensuality, with the desire to be fulfilled, a part of her felt complete and whole, as though missing pieces of herself had at last been found.

"Let me see you," Cabe whispered, placing his hand on her chest. "I won't hurt you, Penny, I swear it. I just want to see you."

"Yes," she said breathlessly. Some would say too much too soon, she thought dreamily, but it would be because they didn't understand. This was Cabe. She and Cabe didn't have to follow the rules of propriety and convention. They had created their own world from the moment they'd met. What they had was, as Cabe said, special and rare.

He drew the zipper down to her waist and brushed

the material away to expose her breasts to his smol-
dering gaze.

"Beautiful," he murmured. "Like ivory velvet. Oh,
Penny," he moaned, and lowered his head to draw
one dusty rose nipple into his mouth.

She gasped from the shock of his mouth on her
breast. He suckled gently, and the tugging was
matched by a demanding pulsing deep within her.
She could feel the flush on her cheeks, could hear
the purr of pleasure that escaped from her throat,
and closed her eyes to savor each new and wondrous
sensation sweeping through her.

Cabe moved to her other breast, and she sank her
fingers into his thick hair, pressing him closer, offering him more. She felt him shudder, his muscles
tighten, and he tore his mouth from her breast and
buried his face in her hair.

"Cabe."

"It's okay," he said, his voice thick with passion.
His breathing was rough as he pulled her robe back
over her breasts with a shaking hand. Then he lifted
his head to gaze at her with smoky blue eyes. "Just
give me a minute, and I'll move."

"No. No, don't go. You feel so good."

"Believe me, so do you, but I've reached my limit
here. A saint I'm not. I've definitely got to call a halt
to this right now."

And a good thing, the part of her that was Penelope thought indignantly. Enough was enough.

It wasn't enough! Penny answered. She wanted
him, all of him. She wanted to be one with Cabe.

No! No! Penelope said.

Yes! Penny insisted.

"I want you, Cabe," she said softly. "I want you to make love to me."

She felt him stiffen, and in the next instant he'd pushed himself off her. He stepped around the coffee table and leaned against the mantel, staring into the fire. Penny struggled to sit up, clutching her robe together with both hands as she stared at his broad, rigid back.

"Cabe?" she said, her voice trembling.

His grip on the mantel tightened. "How do I know? How do I know that I didn't seduce you? How do I know you wouldn't regret it later? I couldn't handle that, Penny. I feel at peace when I'm with you. I can't let anything happen to that. I need it too desperately. It's as though a lifetime has passed since I found you crying in that house. I can't lose you now. I just can't."

She got to her feet and went to him, circling his waist with her arms and resting her head on his back. She simply stood there, loving the feel of him.

He turned in her arms to face her. "Have you had dinner?" he asked.

"Dinner? We're discussing food now?"

"Yes. It's a nice, safe, universal topic." He smiled. "I'll think about my stomach instead of other parts of my anatomy. Why don't you go change and we'll grab a hamburger someplace?"

She shook her head slightly. "You're hard to keep up with. One minute we're . . . Now we're—Grab a hamburger?"

He trailed his thumb over her cheek. "Trust me, okay?"

"I do trust you, Cabe."

"Good. Go put on your jeans."

"All right," she said, smiling up at him. "I just realized that I've never put on my jeans and grabbed a hamburger before."

"Stick with me, kid," he said, wiggling his eyebrows. "I'll teach you all kinds of great stuff."

She batted her eyelashes at him, then began to sashay toward the stairs.

"Is that a fact?" she said over her shoulder, and Cabe laughed.

The cafe on the edge of town was busy, noisy, and smelled like French fries. Cabe was greeted from across the room by a boisterous group of men. He smiled and waved off their invitation to join them. The men hollered complaints about his keeping the pretty lady all to himself.

"Damn right," Cabe muttered. "That booth," he said to Penny, pointing to one toward the back. "It's the only one that doesn't have torn seats."

As Penny slid onto the hard red leather, a huge woman called to Cabe from behind the counter. "Cabe, honey, whatcha want to eat?"

"Hamburgers, fries, and Cokes for two," he said. "How are you, gorgeous Georgia?"

"Still waitin' for you, honey. I'll get your food."

"That's my girl," he said, and sat down opposite Penny. She was leaning over, peering at the wood tabletop. "What are you doing?"

"Reading. There's history on this table, Cabe. Look at all the initials carved in here. B.T. and P.H., D.W. and K.D. Isn't this fun?" She looked up and smiled.

"I wonder where all these couples are now. You know, if they're still together."

"Well, let's see," he said, crossing his arms on the table and looking at the scarred wood. "It's been awhile since I've read the table, you understand, but I'll do the best I can. Oh, hey, there's V.P. and L.T. That's Vicky and Larry. They went steady all through high school. They're married now and have six kids."

"Really?"

He grinned at her. "You know, your eyes are sparkling. You'd think I'd brought you to a five-star restaurant. This is a grungy place, but the food is good."

"And the people are wonderful. Listen to them, Cabe. That's real laughter, not phony, cocktail-party twitter. And you know what else?"

"No, what?" he asked.

"Their clothes. You can't imagine how refreshing it is to see men who are wearing jeans, not worrying about the crease in the slacks of their five-hundred-dollar custom-tailored suits. I'm so tired of looking at five-hundred-dollar suits and chatting with the men who wear them. All they ever talk about is business."

Uh-oh, Cabe thought. He owned five-hundred-dollar custom-tailored suits. In Detroit he was an executive, dedicated to his business. But Penny didn't know that. And Penny wouldn't know that. Not yet. For now he was construction-worker Cabe, pure and simple.

Georgia appeared beside their table. "The plates are hot," she said as she set their food down. "I've got apple pie when you're ready, Cabe. Better watch out for this man, honey," she said to Penny. "He's got quite an appetite. Get the drift?"

Penny blushed, and Cabe laughed as Georgia lumbered off. "She's a great old gal," he said. "I think she's two hundred years old. She was serving me hamburgers and fries when I was in high school."

"And that was at least a hundred years ago," she said, teasing. She gazed with fascination at her hamburger, then leaned across the table toward him. "Cabe, you are about to witness a momentous occasion."

"Oh, yeah?" he said, grinning.

"Indeed. I, Penny, am about to squeeze ketchup from one of those funny red plastic gizmos for the first time in my life. Pay attention. I'd hate to have you miss this."

"You have my undivided attention, ma'am."

With a dramatic flair and an expression of deep concentration on her face, Penny decorated her hamburger with squiggly lines of ketchup. Cabe watched her, his smile growing ever wider.

She was something, he thought. She was so excited, so eager to embrace the world that she was discovering. This was good, all of it. They were just Penny and Cabe, and it was so damn good.

After dinner, during the drive back to Aunt Beth's house, they sang along to the radio. They sang so loudly and so terribly off-key that they kept dissolving into fits of laughter. When Penny remembered her pickup rules and slid across the seat to nestle against him, she was the recipient of a bone-melting kiss.

"I'm not coming in," Cabe said as she unlocked the front door to Aunt Beth's house.

"Why not?" she asked, looking up at him in surprise.

"It wouldn't be a good idea. If we picked up where we left off before, I wouldn't leave. From now on let's take this slow, okay? I don't want anything to happen to us, Penny. Understand?"

"Yes," she said softly. "Cabe, tonight, the cafe, grabbing a hamburger . . . I had a wonderful time. Thank you."

"Well, I gotta tell you," he said, smiling, "you're a first-rate ketchup squirter. Your wrist action was awesome."

"I thought so," she said smugly.

"Ah, Penny." He pulled her into his arms, "I'm the one who's thanking you. You've given me so much. So much." He kissed her on the forehead. "That's it, that peck right there on that spot. I can't handle more than that right now. Go inside. I'll see you tomorrow."

"Good night."

"Good night, my Lucky Penny. Go. I want to know you're safely locked in, and in the meantime I'm freezing to death here."

" 'Bye," she said, then went inside the house and closed the door.

Cabe hunched his shoulders against the cold as he stood staring at the door for a long moment. Then he turned and walked slowly to his truck, deep in thought.

• • •

"Cabe!" Penny yelled. "If you squirt me with that hose once more, I'm going to punch you. And don't say, 'Oops, sorry,' with that innocent expression on your face, because I'm not buying it."

Cabe laughed. "What an attitude. It's not everyone who's allowed to help me wash my truck, you know. You should feel honored."

"What I feel is wet."

He dropped the hose and walked over to her, his gaze lingering on her breasts, which were clearly defined beneath her wet T-shirt. He pulled her into his arms.

"You look sensational," he said. "Feel sensational too. How do you taste? I'll check it out." He kissed her thoroughly. "Sensational."

"That's nice," she said dreamily.

"Back to work," he bellowed, and she jumped in surprise. "I'm on my lunch break, lady, and the mission is a spiffy-clean truck. Lord, this is a great truck. Every guy on the construction crew wishes he had this truck. Quit kissing me, Lucky Penny, and earn your keep."

"Yes, sir," she said, laughing. She plucked a large sponge out of a bucket and smacked it against the truck door.

"Gently," Cabe said. "Treat it with tender, lovin' care."

"Oh, for Pete's sake."

"I've got to do something about your attitude," he muttered, returning to the other side. "You'll appreciate the fine quality of this vehicle someday."

Someday, Penny mused. That word held a hint of a future together, instead of treating this time with

Cabe as temporary. But soon she would have to return to Detroit, to Penelope's world, to being Penelope.

But, oh, not yet, she thought. It was glorious there in Meadow View with Cabe. They were just Penny and Cabe, laughing, talking, touching, kissing.

The day before, Cabe had shown up with a basket of food, and off they'd gone on a real picnic! They'd spread a blanket on a hill, eaten fried chicken, potato salad, and chocolate cupcakes. Cabe had taught her how to find pictures in the clouds, and they'd lain close together, looking at the sky and weaving fantasies of princesses and kings, elves and magical animals. They'd touched on no subject close to reality, but had simply enjoyed each other and the carefree hours. It had been glorious.

Cabe had said good-bye to her on the front porch again, and now here he was on his lunch break once more, giving her the honor—honor?—of helping him wash his truck. And she absolutely adored him.

With every passing minute, Penny knew, her feelings for Cabe were growing stronger. A warmth spread throughout her each time she thought of him or whenever she looked up and found him gazing at her with his incredible blue eyes. And there was another warmth, a throbbing heat that pulsed deep within her, speaking of her desire to become one with Cabe. To make love with Cabe. To join with Cabe in the most intimate sharing between man and woman.

"Hey!" he said suddenly, jarring her from her reverie. "You with the sponge. I'm not paying you to stand around with a silly grin on your face."

A large wet sponge landed squarely on Cabe's nose.

Penny laughed until her stomach ached, and then was quieted by a searing kiss and a promise from Cabe that he'd see her that night after dinner.

" 'Bye," she called as he drove away.

She spent the remainder of the day sorting and packing Aunt Beth's possessions. The front porch was filled with boxes ready to be given to charity. After a long bubble bath, she slipped into her robe, donned her red socks, and ate a supper of soup and a grilled-cheese sandwich. Curling up in the corner of the sofa in front of a roaring fire, she waited for Cabe. His knock came at seven-fifteen.

She opened the door and stepped back to allow him to enter. "Hi," she said softly.

"Oh"—he moaned, taking off his jacket—"you're wearing your Christmas-present outfit. I love that thing."

She wiggled her toes. "Especially the socks, right?"

"Especially," he said, pulling her into his arms, "what's inside the wrapping."

He kissed her with a barely controlled urgency. Without breaking the passionate embrace, he lifted her into his arms and carried her to the sofa, settling onto it with her nestled on his lap. Stopping only long enough to draw air into his lungs, he claimed her mouth again as his fingers inched the zipper of the robe slowly down. His hand closed gently over one bare breast, and Penny whimpered with the sheer pleasure of the feel of his callused hand on her soft skin.

She was consumed by desire, by the pulsing need within her. His arousal was heavy beneath her hips, and she rejoiced in the knowledge that he wanted her as much as she wanted him.

He tore his mouth from hers. "Damn," he said, his voice hoarse with passion. "I'm sorry. I start kissing you and—"

"Cabe," she interrupted. "I want you. I want to make love with you."

"You're killing me, Penny. You know how much I want you, but I have to be sure it's the right time for you. I have to know that you won't be sorry later, that you won't regret it."

"Oh, Cabe, don't you see? Because of you I'm Penny, and that's who I want to be, your Lucky Penny. Yours. Nothing else matters but the world we create when we're together. Love me, Cabe. I won't be sorry. I promise you that." She smiled at him warmly, serenely, as he searched her eyes for reassurance.

"I'm beyond knowing if this is right or wrong," he said. "I want you so damn much."

"And I want you." She slid off his lap and extended her hand to him. "Come with me, Cabe."

She led the way up the stairs and into her bedroom. She stepped away from Cabe and took off her socks, then pulled the zipper of the robe all the way down. The material fell in a pool at her feet, leaving her naked before him. He sucked in his breath as his gaze raked over her; then he stared at the ceiling for a moment as he strove for control. His voice was raspy when he spoke.

"You are the most exquisite woman I have ever seen." He drew his T-shirt over his head and dropped it onto the floor, then reached for the snap on his jeans.

"No, wait," she whispered. She walked over to him and tentatively lifted her hands to his tanned, muscular chest, weaving her fingers through the moist, tawny hair. "Oh, Cabe, you're the one who's exquisite. You're so beautiful." She ran her fingers over his shoulders, then down his arms and back to the hard wall of his chest. She discovered his nipples buried in the curly hair, and felt his muscles tighten under her feathery touch.

"I don't want to rush you, Penny. I really want to take this slow, but I'm hanging on by a thread here. Your touch is heaven, but . . ."

"Yes, I understand," she said. She moved to the bed and flipped back the blankets, then turned to him again.

He joined her and lifted her onto the cool sheets, his gaze sweeping over her again. When he stripped off the rest of his clothes he watched her face as she gazed at every inch of his gleaming body. She smiled and lifted her arms to receive him into her embrace. He stretched out next to her, propped up on one elbow as he splayed his hand on her flat stomach.

"I want this to be perfect for you, Penny. I want, I need, to give you pleasure."

"You will. I know you will."

"I just don't know how much control I have left. I never put it to this kind of test before. If I rush you this time, I'll make it up to you, I promise. We have all night."

"Yes."

"I'm nervous. Can you believe that? It's just so damn important to me that you—"

"Cabe, kiss me."

"Right."

He kissed and touched and caressed her until she was calling to him to quell the fire that raged within her. His mouth paid homage to the lush fullness of first one breast, then the other, and his hand trailed down her body, over the soft flesh of her thighs to the darkness between.

"You're so ready for me," he murmured. "You want me."

"Yes. Yes, please, Cabe."

But still he held back, torturing with his exquisite caresses, until she was tossing her head restlessly on the pillow. His breathing was rough and his muscles were trembling with his effort to control himself.

"Cabe!"

At last he moved over her. He parted her legs with his knee and settled above her.

"This is for you," he said huskily. "All that I am, all that I have, is for you."

He entered her . . . then froze as he stared down at her. "Dammit. Penny, you're a virgin! Why didn't you tell me?"

She slid her hands over his tight buttocks and urged him onward. "Love me, Cabe."

"Can't . . . stop. It's . . . too late."

He thrust deep within her, catching her sharp cry of pain in his mouth as he covered her lips with his. Their bodies began to move together, and to Penny it was magic. It was beyond her wildest fantasies of what this turning point in her life would be like. Her body hummed with pure sensuality as she took all that was Cabe, not even realizing that she was giving in return. She matched the rhythm of his thrusting body and felt herself being lifted away from reality to a place beyond the here and now.

"Cabe! Oh, Cabe, hold me."

"Yes. I'm here. Don't be afraid."

She seemed to shatter into a million brightly colored pieces that were flung into ecstasy.

"Penny!" Cabe called, then shuddered above her, his head thrown back as he strained against her.

Slowly the colors drifted back to make her whole once more. Cabe was heavy upon her, his face buried in her hair. Never had Penny felt so complete, so filled with inner peace and happiness.

Cabe pushed himself up to rest his weight on his arms. He looked down at her passion-flushed face, then groaned and squeezed his eyes closed.

"Dear God," he said. "What have I done?"

Four

As Cabe moved away from her, Penny had a fleeting image in her mind of being a small, fragile crystal vase that was teetering on the edge of a very high shelf. Just moments before, the vase had been filled with a rich, warm gift of beauty, but it was now empty and cold. If the vase fell, it would smash into smithereens and disappear . . . forever.

"Cabe?" she whispered as an uncontrollable trembling swept through her.

He tentatively cradled her cheek in his hand. As he gazed down at her, Penny could see the pain in his eyes, the deep frown that knitted his tawny brows together.

"Why?" he asked, his voice husky. "Why didn't you tell me? You've waited so long to . . . I didn't deserve what you gave to me, Penny. I don't have a damn thing to give you in return."

The vase steadied on the shelf, settling firmly in

place as sunlight spilled over it and warmed it once again.

She smiled. "I'm not sorry, Cabe. I promised you I wouldn't be, and I'm not. It was beautiful, wonderful. I'll cherish what we shared. You gave me everything, don't you see? You gave me yourself. It was Penny and Cabe, just like we said it would be."

"But . . . but what about Penelope? Listen to me, Penny. We've been existing in a fantasy world ever since we met. It was so special, like nothing I've ever experienced, like Alice falling through that rabbit hole and emerging in a place she'd never been in before. There was such peace in our world, a closeness, a bond. I can't even think of words that would describe how beautiful it was."

"Yes, I know."

"I can't believe I went with it all," he continued, shaking his head. "I was running, I guess, escaping from everything I had to face on a daily basis. And there you were, and you were running, too, and it all made sense when we were together. Penny and Cabe, no pasts, no problems, just us."

"We're still just Penny and Cabe," she said softly.

"No." He sank back against the pillow and flung his arm over his eyes. "No, it's over. It's time to face reality. You're Penelope. You just made love with a man you hardly know. You were a virgin, which means you have very strict rules about how you conduct yourself. Yes, you came to me as Penny, but it's Penelope who has to live with herself, pay the piper. Damn. I'm so sorry I did this to you."

Penny pushed herself up against the headboard and tucked the sheet under her arms.

"I refuse to be sorry," she said.

"Dammit!" He sat up and faced her. "Would you wake up? Crawl back out of the rabbit hole and face facts! Who are you?"

"I'm Penny," she said, lifting her chin.

"No, you're Penelope! Penelope who? Say it. Say your name while you're naked in bed with a man you've known for a handful of days."

"Stop it! Don't do this."

"I have to. This is my fault. I'm responsible for what happened here."

"I made my own decision, Cabe," she said, her voice rising.

"No, Penny made it, and I urged—Hell, I practically begged you to stay as Penny, to be my Lucky Penny, because I needed you so damn much. I needed you and what we'd created in our fantasy world. But it's all caught up with us. It's over. The bubble is burst. I have to know if Penelope is going to be able to handle what I've done. *Who are you?*"

"Penny!" she yelled.

"No." He grabbed her shoulders and shook her slightly. "You're Penelope. Penelope who? Say it. Tell me your name.'"

Tears slid down Penny's cheeks. "Penelope Fitzsimmons Chapman!" she cried. "I'm Penelope Fitzsimmons Chapman, vice-president, investment lending, Chapman and Chapman Enterprises of Detroit. The other Chapman is my father, Harold."

"Harold Chapman?" Cabe repeated, astonished. "Harold Chapman! You're *that* Chapman? The daughter of the multimillionaire financial genius? His picture was on the cover of *Time* magazine. He was interviewed on 'Good Morning, America.' He—"

"I know who he is, Cabe," she said, glaring at him.

"Oh. Right. Sure." He shook his head. "Oh, boy."

Damn, Penny thought miserably. Everything was ruined, totally ruined. It had always been this way. The men she met were so in awe of her father, so frightened by the power he possessed, they backed off. They would treat her like royalty for fear that they might have to answer to the king. Cabe looked as stunned as if he'd just discovered she had two noses. Cabe, her Cabe, was acting like all the others. Oh, damn, not Cabe. She was going to cry for the next five years straight.

"Hey," he said, "take it easy, okay?" He slid back down onto the pillow and patted the bed next to him. "Come here."

She sniffled. "What?"

"Come here." He tugged on her hand.

She hesitated a moment, then scooted down next to him, resting her head on his shoulder. He tucked the blankets around them and pulled her even closer to him, gently rubbing her back.

"When you run away from it all, you don't mess around, do you?" he asked softly, his lips resting lightly on her forehead. "I'm beginning to get the picture of who Penelope is. No wonder you were a . . . What I mean is, I understand why you haven't had a serious relationship. A guy would be afraid he'd end up wearing cement shoes in the Detroit River if he messed around with Harold Chapman's daughter."

"Something like that," Penny said, and sniffled again. "My father isn't violent, Cabe, but he does have far-reaching power. Anyone who has shown any interest in me has been thoroughly investigated. Some were fortune hunters, of course. Others who might have been sincere were never good enough by my father's standards."

"And you went with all that?"

"I didn't know how not to. It's a classic case—my father wished he'd had a son, but got a daughter instead. I wanted so desperately to please him. I worked hard in school to prove I was just as smart as a son would have been. He began to accept me, then mold me into being an intricate part of Chapman and Chapman. I didn't question; I just did everything he asked of me."

"Have you been happy all these years?"

"I don't know. I guess so. It's only recently that I've begun to feel trapped and restless, as though I were missing out on part of my life. I tried to push the feelings away, because I didn't want to rock the boat and upset my father's plans. When Aunt Beth died and I came here, it was like having escaped. Then . . . you. And you liked Penny, just ordinary Penny. Oh, Cabe, I can't tell you how wonderful that was, how much it meant to have you accept me just the way you found me. I didn't want to lose you and the world we'd created together. I'd waited too long to have it."

"I understand," he said, still stroking her back. "I really do."

She moved her head back so she could see his

face. "Yes, I think you do understand. Oh, Cabe, please don't be sorry this happened. I know it's over, but don't tarnish any of what we shared by having regrets. Let me have these hours to cherish. Please."

"Over? Us?" He shook his head firmly. "No, I have the whole picture now, so why are you talking as though I'm about to put my pants on and walk out of your life forever?"

"Because I'm Penelope Chapman," she said. "I'm not your Lucky Penny anymore. As you said, it's time to crawl back out of Alice's rabbit hole. Penny is gone."

"Penny," he said, kissing her forehead, "is right here in my arms. My Penny. I'm not giving you up without a fight."

Her eyes widened. "What?"

"You heard me. We deserve a chance to see where all of this leads us. I've said it before and I'll say it again—what we have is special and rare. I believe that you are Penny in your heart, your soul. You are, aren't you? You're my Lucky Penny."

"I—I don't know."

His hand slid up to cup her breast, his thumb trailing back and forth over the nipple until it responded, growing taut, aching for more.

"Tell me," he said, shifting lower to trail a ribbon of kisses down her throat. "Tell me who you want to be." His tongue drew lazy wet circles around the nipple of the other breast. "Say it. I have to know."

"I . . . Oh!" she gasped as hot desire rocketed through her. "I'm Penny. I'm your Lucky Penny. You know that's who I want to be. There can't be any doubt of that in your mind. But it just isn't possible. I—"

"Shh," he said. "No negative thoughts. I am not," he added fiercely, "letting you go. It's time for me to slay the dragons, the demons, inside of me, and now I have a reason to do that. You. I've been wallowing in self-pity for the past six months, feeling so damn sorry for myself. Well, no more. You've turned my life around, and you've knocked me over in the process. We're going to have our chance, Penny. If we're not meant to have something lasting together, *we'll* decide that. But if we are meant to have a future, *no one* is going to stop us."

"Oh, Cabe, it sounds so wonderful, but you have no idea what you're up against."

"Do you trust me?"

"Yes, of course, I do."

"Then we've got it made, sweet Penny."

His mouth captured hers, and she wholeheartedly answered the demands of his lips and tongue. As his hands skimmed over her soft body, hers were tracing the steely muscles of his. Their passions soared again, and everything beyond that room was forgotten. They touched and tasted, kissed and caressed, until their breathing was labored and their hearts thundered.

And then they were one, united. Senses merged as well as bodies, as they sought and found their private place of ecstasy.

Afterward, sated and content, they snuggled together, and Penny yawned.

"Go to sleep," Cabe said, kissing the end of her nose.

"Thank you, Cabe," she mumbled, "for everything."

He held her tightly until her breathing indicated she was asleep, then turned off the light.

"Cabe?"

"I thought you were sleeping."

"I think I was. But it just occurred to me that I still don't know your last name."

He chuckled. "Malone. Now will you go to sleep?"

"Malone. Cabe Malone. Yes, I like that. Good night."

"Good night, Penny," he said quietly. He sifted his fingers through her silken hair and sighed.

Holy smoke, he thought incredulously. Penelope Fitzsimmons Chapman. Harold Chapman was one of the richest, most powerful men in the country. He gobbled up people like Cabe Malone for breakfast. Well, that was just too damn bad. He meant what he'd said. He and Penny would decide if they were meant to have a future together, and Harold Chapman could take a hike.

Oh, really? Cabe thought dryly. Big talk. What was he going to do, storm into Harold Chapman's office and announce he'd bedded the tycoon's virginal daughter? Without, by the way, sir, using any form of birth control. Great. That would probably get him broken kneecaps. He was definitely going to have to think this through and outline some strategy. Without a doubt, he was operating out of his league.

Well, tough. Harold Chapman had better come out of the ether and realize his days of pushing Penelope around were over. She was Penny now. She was his. He'd figure out something. He hoped.

He brushed his lips over Penny's, then closed his eyes. Birth control, he mused. He'd better take charge of that for now. Lord, he'd never even given it a thought earlier. It wasn't like him to be irresponsible about that. But then, he wasn't acting true to form about Penny anyway. She was just so damn important. He'd been a zombie for six months, but thanks to Penny he was alive again. Oh, yes, she was special. And she was his.

He tucked the blankets more securely around her shoulders and drifted off to sleep.

Penny opened her eyes, turned her head to look at Cabe, then sat bolt upright when she saw the empty expanse of bed next to her. The room was flooded with sunlight, the clock on the nightstand said nine-twelve, and Cabe was gone. Then she saw the piece of paper on the dresser. She threw back the blankets and ran across the room, ignoring the ache of muscles she hadn't even known she had.

The note read: "Penny. I'll pick you up at six for dinner. Wear jeans. You're as beautiful asleep as you are awake. CM."

"Oh, how sweet," she said with a sigh, and sank back onto the bed. She'd really done it, she thought. She'd made love with Cabe. Cabe Malone was her lover. It was glorious, and she wasn't sorry. She'd never be sorry.

A chill suddenly swept through her. Cabe was a construction worker, she thought. Her father would go into orbit if he knew what she had done. It made her shudder to think about what he might do. No, not physical violence against Cabe, but subtle trouble for him on his job, wherever he went, to let him know you didn't mess around with Harold Chapman's daughter.

Her father mustn't know about Cabe, she decided. That was the only way to handle this for now. She and Cabe needed time, private time, to discover what they might have together. So far it was perfect, but there was much more to explore. It would have to be here, in Meadow View. She'd keep Aunt Beth's house, minus about half of the furniture, and would tell her father she was using it as a weekend retreat. Could she lie to him? There was only one way to find out. If she and Cabe were discreet in Meadow View and she performed as Prim and Proper Penelope in Detroit, no one would know. They'd have the time they needed. Fine. Yes, marvelous.

As she walked into the bathroom she was humming a happy tune and smiling.

Cabe placed a bouquet of yellow wild flowers on Karen's grave, then moved to stand in front of the stone marker next to it.

"I came to say good-bye, Jason," he said quietly. "I never did, you know, say good-bye, because I couldn't accept that you were gone. Well, I'm facing it now. I'm sorry, Jase, for acting like such a fool all these months. Don't worry about Holly. I'll do what's best for her, I swear it. You should see my Lucky Penny. She's really something." His eyes filled with tears, and an ache nearly closed his throat. "Rest in peace,

Jase," he whispered. "I'm okay now. I sure as hell hope you're with Karen. I really do."

A sudden wind whipped across the cemetery, lifting some of the flowers from Karen's bouquet and scattering them on Jason's grave. Then the wind died down, leaving an almost equal number of the pretty yellow blossoms on Karen's and Jason's graves. Cabe stared at them for a long moment, then turned and slowly walked away.

When Cabe entered the back door of the house, his mother glowered at him.

"Don't say it," he said, raising his hands in a peace-seeking gesture. "I'm scum; I know it. I'm sorry if you were worried, but I'm here and I'm fine. Okay?"

"No."

"Oh." He walked over to the counter and poured himself a cup of coffee.

"Didn't she have a razor you could borrow? You look terrible."

"It's not what you're thinking, Mom," he said, leaning against the counter. "Well, it is what you're thinking, but . . . Well, not really."

"Cabe, I realize you're thirty-four years old and not accountable to me for your actions. However, you are living under this roof, and there is such a thing as thoughtfulness."

"I know, and I'm really sorry. It's bad for Holly to have me come dragging in looking like this too."

"Yes, Holly should be taken into consideration.

You've always managed to get back from your escapades before dawn, until today."

"Escapades," he said, smiling as his eyebrows shot up. "That's a pretty jazzy word there."

"There are others I could use," she said, still glaring at him, "but they're not ladylike. In another era you would have been known as a rogue, young man."

He laughed. "A rogue? Hey, I like the sound of that."

"Oh, Cabe," Martha said with a sigh, "is bed-hopping going to solve your problems?"

"No," he said, serious again and shaking his head. "Mom, the reason I'm so late getting in is because I went to the cemetery. I said good-bye to Jase. It was six months overdue, but I did it."

His mother hugged him tightly. "Oh, thank God. I've been so worried about you."

"I'm asking you to forgive me for what I've put you through. You've had enough to deal with, not to mention my behaving like such a jerk."

"It doesn't matter as long as you've gotten a handle on things now."

"Count on it. Well, I'm off to shower and shave. By the way, I'm bringing someone here for dinner tonight. Her name is Penny, and you'll be crazy about her."

"You're bringing a woman here?"

"Not just a woman, ma'am," he said, grinning at her. "She's my Lucky Penny. Oh, and for now, in case it comes up, I'm just a construction worker. Penny doesn't know about my company yet. Got that? Great. See ya."

"Cabe!"

"Later, Mom. I need a shower," he said, and beat a hasty exit.

"Welcome home, Cabe," Martha said softly to the empty room. Her eyes misted with tears. "Welcome back, my son."

Penny straightened the waistband of her bright blue sweater over her hips, then answered the knock at the door.

"Hello, Cabe," she said, smiling. Black cords, red sweater . . . gorgeous.

"Hi," he said. Blue was great on her, he thought. Her sweater was pretty, and later he'd enjoy every moment of taking it off. "Come here," he said, and pulled her into his arms.

His kiss was long and potent, and Penny's knees felt like wobbly rubber bands when he finally released her.

"Whew," he said. "You're potent stuff, kid. Ready to go?"

"Where are we going?" she asked rather breathlessly.

"My house, for dinner. Well, it's my parents' house. I'm living there at the moment. My mom's name is Martha. She's a great lady. You'll like her."

"I'm going to meet your family?"

"Well, sure. I want them to meet you, too. Look, here it is in a nutshell, okay? I had a twin brother named Jason. He was more than my brother. He was my best friend. Six months ago Jason and his wife, Karen, were killed in an automobile accident."

"Oh, Cabe."

"On the day of the funeral . . ." He moved away from her and began to pace the floor. "On the day of the funeral my father had a stroke. He's partially paralyzed, his speech is affected, and some days he's very confused. My demons, Penny, were the fact that I never really accepted Jase's death . . . until now. And the fact that before my father's stroke he told me that— that the wrong son had died."

"He said that to you? Oh, Cabe, surely he didn't mean it."

"Yes, he did," he said quietly, stopping his pacing. "But it's okay, it really is. The man had a point. Jase was everything I wasn't. My father expected both of us to go into his law firm with him. I didn't want any part of it. Jason was the perfect son. I was a rebel. My father's life centered on the law practice. It and Jason were his pride and joy. Everything just churned around inside of me, Penny. I felt so damn guilty because I was alive and the good boy, the dutiful son, was dead. Does this make sense?"

"Yes. Oh, Cabe, I'm so sorry you've suffered like this."

"Because of you, because I admitted to you I had those demons, I was able to face them. I went to the cemetery this morning and said good-bye to Jase. As for my father . . . " He shrugged. "I can't change anything. What's done is done. But enough of that. Let's see, where was I? Oh, yeah. There's a great old gal at the house, a nurse for my dad, named Tillie. She says I drive her nuts, but she's really crazy about me. And then . . . there's Holly."

"Holly?"

"Jason and Karen's six-year-old daughter. She's mine now, Penny. I'm her legal guardian."

"You're—you're the father, so to speak, of a six-year-old girl?" Penny asked, her eyes wide with surprise.

"Yeah." He shoved his hands into his pockets. "Does that blow your mind?"

"Yes. No. I don't know," she said, throwing up her hands. "You've given me an awful lot to digest all at once, Cabe."

"I guess I did. I just wanted you to have the whole picture before you met Mom. And I wanted to thank you for . . . for being you, that's all. Because of you I'm on the right track again."

"I didn't do anything, Cabe."

"Yes, you did. You gave me the courage to look deep inside myself and face the truths I've been avoiding, running from. It's time I started being a better father for Holly, a better son for my mother. A better man for you. We're a team, you and I. You'll help me be the Cabe Malone I want him to be, and I'll help you be Penny. Not Penelope, but Penny."

"If only it were that simple."

"Piece of cake," he said, grinning at her. "Come over here and kiss me, lady; then I'll take you to meet my crew."

Penny's head was spinning by the time Cabe lifted her into the truck and they drove away from the house. Her dizziness was caused partially by the intensity of his kiss and partially by the impact of all that he had told her.

Cabe was responsible for a six-year-old child, she

thought. Cabe a father? Well, why not? He was probably a wonderful father. It was just startling to be
told suddenly about Holly. And to be told suddenly
that Cabe had lost his twin brother and his sister-in-
law. To be told of Cabe's father's devastating words
on the day of the funeral. No wonder Cabe had been
consumed by demons. He'd been carrying a heavy
load within him.

He had said he lived at his parents' house. Surely
as a construction worker he made enough money to
have his own place. Did he blow every paycheck on
wine, women, and song? No, now, wait a minute.
Holly was at that house. He was probably staying
there because of her. Should she ask him if that was
the reason? Was that rude? She had no idea. She'd
never been in a situation like this before.

He turned into a driveway, and she looked with
interest at the large home set back off the street.

"It's lovely," she said.

"I grew up in this house. It's too big for my folks
now, but my mom says her memories are here. It's a
wonder it's still standing, considering what hellions
Jase and I were."

"Were you identical twins?"

"Yep," he said as he turned off the ignition. "You
can bet we used that fact to our greatest advantage. Man, we pulled some great stuff. Outstanding,
fresh, new, innovative."

She laughed. "You have a strange gleam in your
eye."

"I hope I father identical twins someday. I'd hate
to have all those pranks go to waste. Jason and I
together were brilliant."

"You miss him so very much, don't you?" she asked softly.

He picked up her hand and ran his thumb back and forth over her palm. "Yeah, I miss him," he said, staring at their hands. "I probably always will. We weren't together as much after he married Karen, of course, but the bond was always there." He laughed. "We pulled a stunt on Karen about a month after they were married. We changed clothes, and while Jase hid outside I walked into their kitchen, yelling, 'Honey, I'm home from work.' "

"That's rotten, Cabe Malone."

"Hey, Karen was fantastic. She spotted the difference right off the bat. So she slithers up to me and says, 'I'm hot for your body, baby. Drop your pants and we'll do it on the kitchen table.' I nearly passed out. Jason heard her and came barreling in the back door, just as I took off at a dead run trying to get out of there. I smashed right into him and broke his nose. Karen laughed until she was blue. I swear, I thought we were going to have to call for oxygen for her."

"They sound like they were wonderful," Penny said, squeezing his hand.

"Yep. Let's go in."

Late that night Penny lay close to Cabe in her bed, absently drawing circles on his chest with her fingertip. Their lovemaking had been slow, sweet, and sensuous, and they were contentedly quiet in the aftermath.

"You have a wonderful family," she finally said.

"Yeah, they're top-notch. I know you didn't see my father, but Tillie said he wasn't having a great day."

"I understand. Tillie is marvelous. You tease her unmercifully, you rat."

He chuckled. "She loves it."

"And your mother is so warm and gracious, and she made me feel welcome the moment I stepped into the house. Thank you again, Cabe, for taking me. I had a wonderful time."

"And Holly?" he asked, twining his fingers through her hair. "What did you think of Holly?"

"I have never in my life met such a—" she paused, and immediately felt Cabe tense—"delightful, enchanting child." Cabe released a long sigh. "She's beautiful, Cabe; she looks exactly like you, is smart, funny, and polite. She was so cute, the way she called me Lucky Penny, as if that were my actual name. Do you know that I've never talked to a child for that long? I couldn't believe how well informed she is, how aware of what's happening in the world. I loved it when she giggled behind her hand. She—"

"Whoa," Cabe said, laughing. "You sound like a one-woman fan club for Holly Malone. But seriously, I'm glad you like her. I was at the hospital the night she was born. Lord, she looked weird—all red and wrinkled, and screaming her lungs out. She shaped up fast, though. She's a beauty. And sharp as a tack."

"You're wonderful with her, Cabe. You're firm but fair, and when she talks you listen, really listen, as though what she has to say is very important. My parents . . . Well, when I was small they always gave the impression that I made them nervous, that they were eagerly waiting for me to grow up so we could discuss finance, the stock market, whatever."

"Even your mother?"

"My mother is a math genius. She works with the accounting department of Chapman and Chapman. She doesn't want to waste her time on the mundane, and only gets involved in the complicated, challenging deals my father puts together. Sort of picks and chooses as the mood strikes her. She's happiest when knee-deep in computer print-outs and financial statements. Goodness, listen to me. I sound very critical of my parents. I accepted them as they are years ago. I don't know why I'm getting so vocal now."

"Maybe because I'm listening," Cabe said quietly.

"Yes, maybe because you're listening. I've never really had a friend to talk to before."

"That's another thing you've taught me, Penny. I realize I want to be your friend as well as your lover. I just hope I do okay as a friend. In the past, Jason was always there for me. I've never talked, shared, with a woman. But then, I've never made love with a woman before, either. I've had sex, but I've never made love, until you."

"That's a beautiful thing to say, Cabe."

They were quiet for several minutes, each lost in his own thoughts. They lay close, their hands resting lightly on each other as they shared the same pillow.

"I have some big decisions to make about Holly," Cabe said at last, breaking the comfortable silence. "I know she's happy living with my mother, but my mom has her hands full because of my father. Jason and Karen counted on me to provide a home for Holly, to see to her future, and so far I haven't given that any real thought."

"What do you think you want to do?"

"I don't know. I can't picture Holly living in my apartment in Detroit. There's no yard to play in, no other kids around."

"I see," Penny said. And she finally did see. Cabe had a place to live other than with his parents. He must have signed on with the construction crew in Meadow View to be near Holly. He *didn't* fritter away his paycheck on wine, women, and song. Thank goodness.

Then she frowned. He lived in Detroit? Oh, mercy, she hoped those houses he was working on went up very slowly. For now, they had to be careful and keep their relationship discreetly under wraps in Meadow View. Or under the bed covers, she added, grinning. How naughty of her. For a late bloomer, she was certainly making up for lost time. And she was enjoying every minute of it.

"Well," Cabe said, stretching leisurely, "I won't rush a decision regarding Holly. It's too important, and I want to do what's best for her. I'll have to sort it all through, but what I have to do at this exact point in time is kiss you senseless, then go home."

"I wish you could stay."

"It would be nice to wake up next to you in the morning, but I'd better not. I'll come by on my lunch hour tomorrow. You'll be here, won't you?"

"Oh, yes. I have lots to do."

"But"—he kissed her lightly—"you have to take a break for lunch."

She flicked her tongue over his lips. "A long, long lunch break."

With a groan he claimed her mouth, his tongue delving deep within as his hand gently cupped one of her breasts. She arched into his touch, seeking more, offering more, returning the kiss in total abandon.

It was much, much later before Cabe Malone drove away from the last house on Willow.

Five

When Cabe arrived at Penny's the next day at noon, two men were carrying an overstuffed sofa across the lawn. Their destination was obviously a moving van sitting in the driveway. Just as Cabe reached the front porch two more men walked out of the house toting a glass-front hutch. Behind them emerged a smiling Penny.

"Cabe," she said, her smile growing even bigger. "Your timing is perfect. I've just finished up here."

"Thank you, ma'am," one of the men said. "You've been very generous."

"You're most welcome," Penny said. "Good-bye." She looked at Cabe again. "Come in and see what I've done."

Cabe entered the house and glanced around. The living room held a normal amount of furniture, arranged in attractive groupings. It looked homey and cozy, he thought.

"Very nice," he said. "So what's the plan? You figure it will look better when you sell it?"

"Oh, no," she said. "I'm not going to sell it. This is going to be my weekend retreat, or so I'll tell my father. It's actually for us, Cabe, when I come up from Detroit. I can be here by Friday night each week, and I won't have to leave until late Sunday. Or maybe Monday morning, if I get up real early. Even when the snow comes I shouldn't have any problem. That road is always kept clear, and I can whiz right through and—"

"Hold it," he said, raising his hand. "You're going too fast for me. Let me see if I have this straight. I'm to stay here in Meadow View and wait for you to come up on the weekends?"

"Well, yes. We need time together, Cabe, just as you said. A chance to know what we might have together. What better way to do that than right here? My father won't question my getting away from Detroit on weekends." She paused. "You don't look very happy. I thought you'd be pleased."

"Pleased?" He frowned as he raked a hand through his hair. "No, not even close. Penny, the last time I sneaked around like this was when I kissed Mary Ellen Singleton in the coatroom at a junior-high dance. I have no intention of being safely stashed away in Meadow View during the week while you're being Penelope, and waiting for you to turn into Penny on Fridays and come to me. No. No way."

"But—"

"No." He sliced his hand through the air for silence. "It would still be a fantasy world, don't you see? Penny and Cabe, no last names, having a wild time in bed in their secret hideaway every weekend."

She narrowed her eyes. "Don't get crude."

"Well, hell, what do you expect me to say? Heaven forbid the great Harold Chapman should know that his ever-so-proper Penelope is making it with a construction worker, a blue-collar, middle-class bum. It's probably more than Penelope Fitzsimmons Chapman can deal with in the light of day. Penny thinks it's great, but Penelope? Penelope intends to keep said lover under wraps, so he won't embarrass her in any way. No soap, lady. I'm not playing this game."

"Darn it, Cabe, this isn't a game! I'm trying to give us the time we need, without my father's interference. You've misinterpreted everything."

"Have I? I don't think so. You're still doing your Alice-down-the-rabbit-hole number. You listen to me, Penny. I see you in Detroit as well as in Meadow View or I don't see you at all."

"What?" she whispered. "That's crazy. My father will—"

"I don't give a damn about your father," he roared. "What I *do* give a damn about is my pride. I won't be kept on a back burner, hidden in a closet until you decide to take me out and play with me. Yes, we need some time together, but it has to be up-front and honest, or it isn't worth anything. When are you going back to Detroit?"

"This afternoon. I have work stacking up that I have to attend to. But I was planning to come back on Friday evening, Cabe. I thought we could have the whole weekend together."

"There's nothing wrong with two people shutting

the door on the world for the weekend, Penny. But it *is* wrong if they've pretended that the outside world and the other person don't exist during the week. *I* don't think we have anything to hide. I'm apparently alone in that opinion. Harold Chapman may tell you what to do, but he doesn't tell me."

"Cabe, you don't know him," Penny said frantically. "When he finds out about you he'll have you investigated. He'll discover that you're only a construction worker and—"

"Only a construction worker," he interrupted, his voice ominously low. "And obviously not good enough for his daughter. What about me, the man, how I think, what my values are? Don't they count for anything?"

"Not to him."

"And to you? What about Penelope? How does she measure the worth of her men?"

"Cabe, stop it."

"Who are you really hiding me from, Penny? Your father? Or from Penelope's world? Would I embarrass you in front of your high-society friends?"

"That's not fair. My father has power and connections. He could find a way to get you fired from your job and make sure you don't work on any other crew. If we *are* to have a future together, then we'll face Harold Chapman as a couple. In the meantime, don't put yourself at risk."

"Nice spiel, but I'll pass. I won't be hidden away up here and wait like an obedient puppy for you to arrive on Friday nights. Okay, go on to Detroit; turn into Penelope again. But when you come back this

Friday, you'd better have your head on straight and understand that I won't do it this way."

"Oh, Cabe, please," she said, taking a step toward him.

"Nò." He raised a hand to halt her. "Just stay over there. If I start kissing you I'll probably agree to anything. Go back to Detroit, Penny. See how Penelope feels about what you've done here with me. Find out how much that world means to you, because you could very well be laying it all on the line if you and I make a stand. Get in touch with yourself, because you're messing around in the big leagues. I won't be your weekend lover. You'd better remember that." He turned toward the door. "I'll see you."

"Please don't leave, not like this."

"You don't offer me any other choice. If I stay, I'll make love to you. The next thing I know, I'll probably be bobbing my head up and down, promising to hide out here like a good little boy until you can fit me into your schedule. I'm definitely leaving now. It will give you extra time to think, and from where I'm standing you could use it." He left the house, closing the door roughly behind him.

"Cabe!" she called. "Cabe Malone, you are a hard-headed, stubborn man!" And he was also gone, she thought, blinking against her tears.

She sank onto a chair and stared at the door, willing it to open and for Cabe to stride back into the house. He'd pull her into his arms, kiss her until she couldn't breathe, then say he'd acted hastily, that her plan for them to have their weekends together in Meadow View was the best way to handle this relationship for now.

"alluring"..."inspiring"...
"irresistible"...

Loveswept

EXAMINE 6 LOVESWEPT NOVELS FOR

15 Days FREE!

Turn page for details

America's most popular, most compelling romance novels...

Loveswept

Here, at last...love stories that really involve you! Fresh, finely crafted novels with story lines so believable you'll feel you're actually living them.

Read a Loveswept novel and you'll experience all the very real feelings of two people as they discover and build an involved relationship: laughing, crying, learning and loving. Characters you can relate to... exciting places to visit...unexpected plot twists...all in all exciting romances that satisfy your mind and delight your heart. *One book FREE every month.*

And now you can be sure you'll never, ever miss a single Loveswept title by enrolling in our special reader's home delivery service. A service that will bring you all six new Loveswept romances each month for the price of five—and deliver them to you before they appear in the bookstores!

Examine 6 Loveswept Novels for

15 Days FREE!

To introduce you to this fabulous service, you'll get six brand-new Loveswept releases not yet in the bookstores. These six exciting new titles are yours to examine for 15 days without obligation to buy. Keep them if you wish for just $12.50 (that's six books for the price of five) plus postage and handling and any applicable sales tax.

BUSINESS REPLY MAIL

FIRST-CLASS MAIL   PERMIT NO. 2456   HICKSVILLE, NY

Postage will be paid by addressee

Loveswept

Bantam Books
P.O. Box 985
Hicksville, NY 11802

But the door didn't open, nor did Cabe return, and tears began to slide down Penny's cheeks. Cabe wasn't being reasonable, she decided. He was acting all macho and putting his misplaced pride before common sense. An obedient puppy indeed. What an asinine thing to say. There was absolutely nothing wrong with the two of them spending the weekends together in Meadow View.

Or was there? she wondered, brushing the tears from her cheeks. Was she subconsciously trying to protect Penelope's world in case her glorious existence as Penny crumbled into dust? Penny was so fragile and new, like a baby taking her first steps and unwilling to let go of a familiar, safe hand. Had her grand plan been nothing more than a way to have her delicious, beautiful cake of Cabe and leave untouched her plain, drab, undecorated existence as Penelope?

"That's really stinky, Penny Chapman," she said aloud. "No wonder Cabe was screaming his head off."

No, now, wait a minute, she thought. She was trying to shield Cabe from the wrath of her father. Cabe could very well pay forever for a brief fling with the powerful man's daughter. Brief fling? Lord, how depressing. She didn't want brief, and it wasn't a fling. It was special and real, and held promises of a future with a unique, warm, magnificent, loving man.

Was she falling in love with Cabe Malone? she wondered. How would she know? She was so inexperienced in the workings of the heart. She might not recognize love if it punched her in the nose! She was only now discovering who she was as a woman, as Penny, thanks to Cabe's appearance in her life. How did love make its presence known?

"This is terribly confusing," she said, pressing her hands to flushed cheeks. Cabe was right, she realized. She needed to think, to sort things through. She had to crawl back out of Alice's rabbit hole and return to Detroit, face reality, view through Penelope's eyes all that had happened to Penny. And she had to keep telling herself that despite how it sounded, she wasn't schizophrenic. This Penny/Penelope business was becoming nuts!

With a sigh she got to her feet and went slowly up the stairs to pack her suitcase.

Penny stood just inside the door of her apartment and glanced around, as if seeing her home for the first time. She set her suitcase on the floor and walked slowly forward, stopping to run her fingers over the back of the white velvet sofa. She'd lavishly decorated the apartment in the same color scheme throughout— white with accents of dusty blue and rose.

And as of that very moment she hated it.

It was cold, she decided. Cold and sterile. It held none of the warmth and coziness of Aunt Beth's home, and had never had the aroma of cinnamon wafting through the air. Oh, it was stylish. She'd spared no expense in furnishing it, and *House Beautiful* had even asked to feature it. But it looked like a display in a store, as though no one lived there.

She glanced down at her jeans, then at the sofa. No one in jeans had ever sat on that sofa. No one in faded jeans and a T-shirt and in need of a haircut had ever stepped inside this apartment. She'd entertained only the wealthy or soon-to-be wealthy, with their designer clothes and styled-to-perfection hair. With her own expensive outfits and plastic smile and catered food, she'd been the perfect hostess. She'd laughed at all the proper times, discussed the latest theater performance, lamented the state of the stock market. She'd played out the role of Penelope Fitzsimmons Chapman and never questioned it, except for those fleeting moments of restlessness. She'd never questioned the way she lived her life . . . until now. Until Cabe.

She missed him.

She wanted him there, right then. She wanted to kiss him, to touch him, to make love with him.

She wanted to be Penny.

She wrapped her arms around her waist as a shiver ran through her, and once again studied the large room. So cold and so quiet, she thought. And so empty . . . without Cabe.

Tomorrow she'd go to Chapman and Chapman as Penelope. She'd see her father, and it would be business as usual. She knew he'd suspect nothing, would see no change in his efficient, organized daughter. But she *was* different, and she gloried in the knowledge. She'd shed the cocoon of her sheltered past and emerged at last as a woman. She'd given her body to a man, and she'd chosen well.

Was this love? she wondered again. Was this ache of loneliness for Cabe, the almost desperate need to have him near, truly love? Oh, if she only knew. And if she only knew the depth of Cabe's feelings for her. And if she only knew what the future held.

"I sure don't know very much," she said, throwing up her hands.

Chapman and Chapman Enterprises was housed on the entire top floor of a high-rise building in Detroit's business district. The thick carpeting and expensive furnishings in the reception area caused visitors to speak in hushed tones, as they became instantly aware of the affluence surrounding them.

When Penny stepped off the elevator the next morning she glanced around, much as she had in her own apartment, as if seeing the offices for the first time. Swanky but boring, she decided. But then, *she* looked swanky but boring too. Her attractive gray suit was an original, and her pink blouse was raw silk. Her hair was twisted into a tight chignon at the nape of her neck, and her freckles had been carefully covered by makeup. She was the picture of efficiency, wealth, and authority. Swanky but boring.

She nodded to the receptionist, then walked down the carpeted hall to her office. Her secretary, a dauntingly organized woman, who always addressed her as "Ms. Chapman," welcomed her back and handed her a large stack of pink message slips. Mumbling something about having to get started on returning the calls, Penny hurried into her corner office. Once inside, she closed the door and leaned against it, then shut her eyes and drew in a steadying breath.

She didn't want to be there! she screamed silently.

This was Penelope's office, those were Penelope's messages, this was Penelope's world.

And she was Penny!

She opened her eyes. Sunlight streamed in the floor-to-ceiling windows, dancing over the glass-and-chrome desk, the silver-gray easy chairs, the glass-top coffee table. A glass-and-chrome sideboard held the finest of liquors and crystal glasses and a state-of-the-art stereo system. Off to the right there was a gleaming black-and-white bathroom.

It was all first class, and cold, she thought. It was where Penelope Fitzsimmons Chapman had come every day for years without a second thought. Where Penelope had performed her job with awesome expertise in the manner befitting a Chapman.

But Penny didn't want to be here.

On trembling legs she walked to the desk and sank heavily into the butter-soft leather chair behind it. She pressed her fingertips to her now-throbbing temples as one image flitted through her mind. Cabe.

Cabe, with his beautiful blue eyes and unruly sun-streaked hair, his broad shoulders and lean hips, the cleft in his chin, and his flashing smile. Cabe, who had suffered such pain when he lost his brother, then who had slain his inner demons created by that death and his father's harsh words. Cabe, who touched gently the battered soul of the child left in his care. Cabe, who had reached out his hand and beckoned to Penny.

And she had gone.

Accepting all that he was, all that he offered her in his honest, down-to-earth way, she had placed her hand in Cabe's, trusting him, wanting him, and, even more, acknowledging her need for him. He made her whole, not just in body, when they made love, but in spirit, in the very essence of her being. With Cabe, only with Cabe, could she reach the full potential of her womanhood and of herself.

She loved him.

There, in the quiet, sunlit room, Penny Chapman knew she was in love with Cabe Malone. What had been so confusing was now perfectly clear. It was Penny and Cabe. Together.

The buzzing of the intercom on her desk startled her, and she gasped. Blinking once, slowly, she pulled herself from her reverie and pressed the button.

"Yes?"

"Clifford Meredith on line one," her secretary said crisply.

"Thank you," she said, then sighed. She *really* didn't want to be here! She lifted the receiver to her ear. "Clifford? I have good news. We can loan you the two million at the variable rate cited in my proposal. When you come by to sign the papers, I'll have a check waiting for you."

"Fantastic. I knew you'd work it out, Penelope."

Penny! she ached to scream at him.

"You're a marvel," Clifford went on. "How about lunch to celebrate?"

"I really can't. I just got back, and I'm up to my elbows in work."

"Well, dinner next week, then. I'll be by this afternoon to sign the papers and get my check."

She had a suggestion for what he could do with that check, she thought, smiling. Oh, not nice. Not nice at all. "Fine," she said, swallowing her laughter. "Good-bye, Clifford."

" 'Bye, Penelope."

She rolled her eyes and hung up the phone. "Penny," she said to the receiver.

With a resigned sigh she started sifting through the stack of messages.

Harold Chapman looked at the man seated in the chair opposite his massive hand-carved desk.

"You understand," he said brusquely, "that I don't see anyone without an appointment. I'm only doing this because your father is Matthew Malone. I was very sorry to hear about Matt's stroke and the death of your brother. Matt and I go back a long way. His illness made me painfully aware that time passes very quickly. We, myself included, find ourselves older than we realized, all of a sudden. Give Matt my best." He paused. "So, Cabe, what can I do for you?"

Cabe looked directly at Harold Chapman while resisting the urge to tug his strangling tie loose from his neck. Lord, he hated ties, he thought. And the three-piece suit was really uncomfortable. But along with his expertly cut hair, they created the image he wished to present. He cleared his throat.

"I'm in love with your daughter."

Amazing, Cabe thought. It was absolutely amazing how Harold Chapman's face turned from a normal color to beet red in a matter of seconds.

"You're . . ." Harold stopped to draw in a great gulp of air. "You're in love with my daughter?"

"Yes, sir, I am," Cabe said pleasantly. "And being

an old-fashioned type of guy, I thought I would meet with you privately and inform you of that fact." He took a card from his breast pocket and leaned forward to place it on the desk. "My card. Since I know you'll want to have me fully investigated, that will save you some time. I'm the president and owner of Malone Construction Company. I don't plan on providing you with my financial statement, because it's none of your business how much I make, nor does my net worth have anything to do with my love for Penny. You'll dig up the information you want, but my assistance goes no further than giving you my card."

Harold lunged to his feet and leaned forward, his hands flat on the desk, his face still flushed. "Who in the hell do you think you are?"

Cabe slowly pushed himself to his feet and met Harold's angry stare. "I know exactly who I am. I'm Cabe Malone, son of Martha and Matthew, brother of the late Jason Malone. I'm the man, Mr. Chapman, who intends to marry your daughter."

Harold opened his mouth to speak, but when nothing came out, he smacked the button on his intercom.

This was it! Cabe thought. This was where Chapman called in the gorillas who broke kneecaps and took measurements for cement shoes! He had to stay loose. His and Penny's future was at stake here. If he lived that long.

"Leslie," Harold roared into the intercom, "tell Penelope I want to see her in my office right now. Then hold my calls."

Uh-oh, Cabe thought. Not good. He'd been counting his lucky stars when he'd made it all the way into Harold's office without Penny's seeing him. Now they were going to have a three-way confrontation that would probably register an eight on the Richter scale. Get it together, Malone, he told himself. A helluva lot was riding on the next few minutes. And it would help immensely if he didn't pass out cold. He'd planned this all, the day Penny had left Meadow View. After he'd cooled down, that is. He could pull this off. He had to!

The door opened, and he turned to see Penny walk briskly into the office. No, he thought, that wasn't Penny, that was Penelope, complete with uniform and an uptown hairdo. Yes, she was Penelope Fitzsimmons Chapman, all right. But he knew what was beneath that overwhelmingly professional facade. Penny was there. His Lucky Penny. And he loved her.

"Good morning, Harold," she said. "You wanted to see—" Her glance fell on Cabe, and she stopped dead in her tracks. Her eyes widened as her gaze raked over him from head to toe. "Cabe?" she whispered.

"Hi," he said, giving her a dazzling smile. "How are you?" He crossed his arms loosely over his chest and continued to smile at her.

Penny walked slowly forward, doing yet another thorough scrutiny of Cabe.

"What are you doing here?" she asked in a strange, squeaky voice. "Where's your hair? Why are you wearing that suit?"

"Should I answer those in order, or just pick and choose?"

"Penelope," Harold said sternly, "this young man

had the audacity to come into my office and tell me that he—"

"Cut," Cabe said. "I should be the one to tell her. I haven't had the chance to do that yet."

"Tell me what?" Penny asked. She looked at Cabe, then at her father, then at Cabe again.

"That I love you and I want to marry you," Cabe said, his smile returning to hundred-watt status.

"I beg your pardon?" she sank onto a chair as her knees turned to jelly. "You what? And you want to do what?"

"I love you and I want to marry you. I would have preferred a romantic setting for a declaration and proposal, but it didn't work out that way. Sorry 'bout that. Anyway, I came to inform your father, because that's how they did these things in the old days and I thought it was a rather nice touch."

"Pen-el-ope!" Harold roared. "Who is this man?"

Cabe sighed. "I already told you. I'm Cabe Malone— it's there on my card—son of Martha and Matthew, and—"

"Shut up," Harold said. Cabe shrugged and shut up. "Penelope?"

"Penny," Cabe interjected. Harold glared at him. Cabe shrugged again and shut up again.

"Well?" Harold said, looking at his daughter.

"Who is this man?" she repeated. Think of something, she told herself frantically. Stall. Lord, Cabe looked beautiful, as if he'd stepped off the page of a fashion magazine. But where was his hair? He loved her? He wanted to marry her?

"Penelope," Harold said, "I'm running very short of patience."

"What?" She turned to her father. "I—I've never seen this man before in my life," she said in a rush of words. Oh, good Lord, what a stupid thing to say.

Cabe laughed. "That's rich. I love it."

"Shut up," Harold said.

"Right," Cabe said. "Got it."

"I don't believe you," Harold said to Penelope.

She threw up her hands. "I don't either."

"I will ask this only once more," Harold said, picking up Cabe's card. "What is your relationship to"—he glanced at the card—"Cabe Malone, president and owner of Malone Construction Company?"

Uh-oh, Cabe thought, watching Penny get slowly to her feet as she stared at him. He was in big trouble. This was one angry woman. He could see the fury building within her. Her eyes were flashing, her cheeks had turned pink, her freckles had popped out from beneath that glop she was wearing to cover them up. She was gorgeous. And mad as hell.

"President and owner," she said, her words precise and measured, "of Malone Construction Company? You're not a shaggy-haired construction worker in tight jeans?"

"Well, sometimes I am," he said. "I get cabin fever in my office and I like to go on a site for a while, to get it on with the down-and-dirty. You know what I mean?"

"Why didn't you tell me?" she yelled. "You lied to me!"

"I certainly did not," he said indignantly. "I just hadn't gotten around to informing you of a simple little detail, that's all."

"Simple? Simple! I thought you were a . . . And it turns out you're a . . . I call that lying, Cabe Malone."

"It is not."

"Shut up!" Harold shouted. "I demand that you explain yourself, Penelope. What is your relationship with this man?"

She spun around, eyes flashing. "You demand? Demand? Okay, Harold, listen up. This man"—she pointed at Cabe—"is my lover!"

Uh-oh, Cabe thought one more time. Uh-oh, uh-oh, uh-oh.

"Oh, dear heaven," Penny whispered, her hands flying to her cheeks. "What have I done?"

Harold sank into his chair with a thud. "Your . . . lover?"

"I don't feel well," she said.

"Let me help you into a chair, honey," Cabe said, starting toward her.

"Don't touch me." She smacked his hand away. "You're a phony, Cabe Malone. You said you were one thing and it turns out you're something else." Her eyes filled with tears. "I thought our relationship was based on honesty, that what we had was so special and real. I adored your shaggy hair and faded jeans, but that's not even who you are."

"Yes, it is," he said quietly. "That was Cabe. That was the Cabe you accepted just the way he was. That meant as much to me as my accepting Penny as *she* was had meant to you. I'm sorry I didn't tell you about my company. I should have, I realize that, but now you know, and it shouldn't change anything. We're still Penny and Cabe."

"No," she said, shaking her head. "Look at you."

She flapped her hand at him. "That's a custom-made suit. I hate it. That's a salon haircut. I hate that too."

"My body underneath hasn't changed," he said, grinning at her. "You're crazy about that."

"Aaagh!" she screamed. "Shut up."

"You Chapmans sure like that phrase," he said, rolling his eyes.

"I've had enough of this," Harold said, pounding the desk with his fist. "I want you out of here, Malone. I want you out of this office and away from my daughter. Am I making myself clear?"

Cabe flattened his hands on Harold's desk and leaned close to the older man. "I don't give a tinker's damn what you want, Chapman," he said. "You can do your worst, but you won't stop me. I'm in love with Penny. She's mine. Understand? *Penny is mine!*"

"The hell you say," Harold roared. "I'll break you, Malone. No one takes something from me that I'm not ready to give. Penelope belongs to me. She always has, and she will until I decide differently. You're finished in this town. You can kiss Malone Construction good-bye. Get this straight once and for all. Penelope is a Chapman. She does as I say. *She belongs to me!*"

"No!" Penny cried, nearly choking on a sob. "You can both go straight to hell."

Cabe spun around to face her. "Penny—"

"No." She began to back away. "You're both the same. You're arguing about me like two dogs haggling over a bone. Well, no more." Tears slid down her cheeks. "I'm not your Penny, and I'm not your

Penelope. I'm just me, alone, and that's how I want it. I don't *belong* to anyone but myself. Stay away from me, both of you. Stay out of my life!" She turned and ran from the office.

"Penny!" Cabe yelled.

"Penelope!" Harold echoed.

There was no answer.

"Oh, damn," Cabe said, running his hand down his face.

"I've never seen her like this," Harold said. "I've never seen her cry. She's always so calm and in control."

"Like a good little Chapman?" Cabe asked, turning to face Harold again. "Like a programmed robot would be closer to the mark. You don't even know her, Chapman. I've seen her cry before today, and I've heard her laugh. She's Penny, with her hair loose and free. Penny, who wears jeans and rides in pickups. She's Penny, who accepted me as I was, not caring that I was a blue-collar construction worker."

"Malone, I—"

"No, listen, just listen. I love that woman. She's my life, my reason for being. You spoke of my father's stroke and how it made you realize that time was passing. You're going to wake up one of these days and discover that you're an old man who never knew, really knew, his own child. Well, *I* know her, and I'm not going to lose her. You can hassle me, use your power to destroy my company. But I won't be stopped. I'm going to fight with every breath in my body to win Penny's love."

Harold sank into his plush leather chair and stared

at Cabe. Seconds ticked into minutes, and the silence hung like an oppressive weight in the air. Cabe never took his gaze from Harold's. He knew Harold was studying him, measuring him with an invisible yardstick that might determine his fate. But he didn't care. Nothing mattered except Penny.

"Cabe," Harold said finally, his voice oddly husky, "make her happy. That's something her mother and I apparently never did. Put the sparkle in Penelope's eyes. Give her reason to laugh right out loud. Love her, son, with the same determination you just used to go against me."

"I intend to," Cabe said. "And, Harold, her name is Penny."

"Penny," Harold said, smiling.

"My Lucky Penny," Cabe said quietly, turning to stare at the open doorway that Penny had run through. "And I love her."

Six

As he had done every Sunday for the past four months, Cabe stopped his truck in front of the last house on Willow. He crossed his arms over the steering wheel and leaned forward to get a full view of the dark building. He allowed his imagination to run wild, picturing the door bursting open and Penny running out to greet him. But as every Sunday before, there was no Penny.

He sighed and leaned back in the seat. Unbelievable, he thought dismally. It was unbelievable that the finest detectives in the country, hired by Harold Chapman, had not been able to find Penny in four months. It was as though she had disappeared from the face of the earth. If it weren't for the telephone call she had made to her mother on Christmas, there would be no clue that she was even alive.

Cabe hit the steering wheel. Dammit, where was she? Lord, he missed her. He wanted to see her, to hold her, to tell her how much he loved her. He knew that by closing his eyes he could conjure her image, hear her laughter, see her smile. And with the vision would come the memory of her tears shed that day in her father's office, and her flight from the two men who had hurt her so badly.

He turned the key in the ignition and drove slowly away from the house. Harold Chapman's health was failing, Cabe knew it, and he couldn't do anything about it. The man was obsessed with finding Penny, and neither slept nor ate properly. Cabe constantly urged Harold to try to relax, but Harold wouldn't listen either to Cabe or to Penny's mother.

Cabe found it odd that during these past four months, Harold had turned to him as a father would to a son. There was a bond between them that had never existed between Cabe and his actual father. He shared with Harold the goal of finding Penny, the woman they loved, each in his own way.

"Come home, Penny," Cabe said aloud. "I'm so damn sorry. I never meant to hurt you, I swear it. I just want to love you, that's all."

He pulled into the driveway of his mother's home and got out of the truck. The snowman he had helped Holly build the day before was rapidly melting in the winter sun, and the carrot they had used for a nose was drooping at a precarious angle. The thought of Holly brought a smile to Cabe's lips, and he quickened his step. He came up to Meadow View every weekend to be with Holly, and their time together refreshed his aching soul and renewed his spirit, enabling him to face another week of grueling work at Malone Construction.

Inside the house he shrugged out of his sheepskin jacket and hung it in the front closet. He rubbed his hands together to warm them, then looked up as his mother hurried down the hall toward him.

"What's wrong?" he asked, stiffening.

"You're to call Harold Chapman immediately," Martha said, her eyes filling with tears. "Oh, Cabe, the detectives found her. They've found Penny!"

"Dear God," he said, swaying slightly. "Is . . . is she all right?"

"Yes," Martha said, smiling through her tears. "They didn't approach her, as Harold instructed, but they saw her, and she appears to be fine."

"Where?" Cabe asked, his voice thick with emotion. "Where is she?"

"Florida."

"Florida," he repeated. Penny! Oh, dear Lord, they'd found his Penny.

"Cabe," Martha said sharply.

He jerked in surprise. "What?"

"Come out of your fog and go call Harold. Now."

"Yes." He pulled his mother into his arms and hugged her tightly. "I love her, Mom. Somehow, *somehow*, I've got to convince her of that."

"You will," Martha said, ignoring the tears streaming down her face. "Go to her, Cabe. Go to your Penny."

He gave her an extra squeeze, then ran down the hall and into the den. A few moments later he was talking to Harold Chapman.

Penny quickened her step as the misty rain grew

chillier and was whipped along the beach by a sudden wind. Clouds had been building when she'd started off on her walk, and she'd carried a thigh-length cardigan sweater over her arm. She'd soon buttoned it over her blouse and jeans as the temperature dropped, but the rain had started before she could return to the house. She was thoroughly soaked, and had visions of a crackling fire in the hearth and a long, leisurely bubble bath.

As the house came into view, she brushed her streaming hair from her eyes and started to jog, aware that her teeth were beginning to chatter. The intensity of the rain increased, and she squinted against the swirling onslaught.

And then she stopped.

A man had risen from the bottom step of the stairs leading up to her house and was walking slowly toward her.

It was Cabe.

A sob caught in her throat as she watched him approach. The sound of her own thudding heart drowned out the noises of the rain and the waves crashing against the shore. She wanted to turn and run away. She wanted to rush forward and fling herself into his arms. She wanted to scream at him to leave her alone. She wanted to hold fast to him and never again let him go. Her thoughts tumbled together in a jumbled maze as unshed tears burned her eyes and caused an ache in her throat. She couldn't move, could hardly breathe, as Cabe came closer. And closer.

He stopped about three feet away from her, seemingly oblivious to the cold, driving rain. As their eyes met, time ceased to exist. Then he drew a deep, shuddering breath that she could almost feel in the depths of her own body.

"Penny."

Oh, God, she thought. Such pain in his voice, such anguish. He looked so tired. Her beautiful Cabe was so tired. She wanted to comfort him, to hold him and tell him that she loved him, would always love him. She'd . . . No, she had to be strong, to listen to her head and not her heart. This was Cabe, who had lied to her, had shown himself to be just like her father. He wanted to own her, to possess her as he would an object he considered of value. She belonged to no one but herself. She'd fought too hard for her newfound freedom, and she wasn't giving it up. Not even for Cabe.

She lifted her chin. "You found me," she said, thankful her voice was steady.

Cabe studied her face for a long moment, then shoved his hands into the pockets of his windbreaker. He drew himself up to his full height, looked down at the ground as though gathering his inner strength, then met her gaze again.

"Your father hired detectives. It took them all this time to discover where you were."

"I see. And Harold let you come instead of himself?"

"He . . . understood. Penny, you're soaked to the skin, and it's cold out here."

"I like being cold and wet," she said, lifting her chin even higher. Oh, how childish. What a ridiculous thing to say.

"Well, *I* don't." Malone, he told himself, you've got a helluva road to go here. Lord, she was beautiful.

Even soaked, with her luscious hair plastered down, Penny was the most exquisite woman he'd ever seen. He was aching to pull her into his arms and smother her lips with his, to mold her body to his and feel her softness against him. He wanted to touch and taste every inch of her, to make love to her through the hours of the night. He'd declare his love over and over, and she'd believe that he meant it. And then she would say that she loved him in return. He was dreaming, and all that was going to come of it was a case of pneumonia.

Penny shivered.

"Come on," he said. "This is nuts. Let's go inside, okay? We have to talk."

"There's nothing to talk about."

"We'll begin with talking about getting warm and dry."

"Well, I suppose," she said. She started forward, then stopped, waiting for Cabe to move out of her way. He raised his hands in a gesture of peace and stepped sideways. "Thank you, Mr. Malone," she said, and strode past him with all the dignity she could muster, considering she must have looked like a drowned rat.

Cabe smiled and fell into step three paces behind her.

The house at the top of the steep stairs was expensively furnished and invitingly warm. Penny and Cabe entered through the kitchen, then stood dripping water on the floor.

"Do you have dry things?" she asked, turning to look at him. She was struck again by how handsome and tired and wonderful he looked.

"My suitcase is in the car."

"Well, you can shower and change, but then you'll have to leave, Cabe."

"You go get out of your wet clothes. I'll meet you in the living room in a bit."

"Did you hear me say you'll have to leave?"

"I heard you, Penny," he said quietly.

Their eyes met—sad eyes, searching eyes. Then Penny tore her gaze from Cabe's and hurried from the room.

"Helluva road to go," he said under his breath, "and worth every minute." Lord above, how he did love that woman.

Penny stood under the warm water of the shower. She told herself her trembling was because she was chilled, then admitted that she was lying. She blanked her mind and refused to think.

After blow-drying her hair into shiny waves that tumbled past her shoulders, she floated a soft russet-colored caftan over her head, then pulled on green-and-white striped knee socks. The socks clashed with the rich material of the caftan, but she didn't care.

When she entered the living room, Cabe was setting the screen in front of a roaring fire in the fireplace. Her gaze roamed over him, drinking in every detail of his thick, damp hair, his wide shoulders in the black sweater, the way his black cords lovingly hugged his buttocks, hips, and legs. Tingling fingers of desire crept throughout her, but she ignored them, wishing they hadn't created the flush she knew was on her cheeks.

Cabe turned and saw her. "I started some coffee. I hope that's all right."

"Yes, of course," she said, snapping on a light. "It's awfully dark for midafternoon. The storm, you know. It made it dark. I enjoy watching storms as they roll in over the water."

"Penny."

"The weather changes very quickly here sometimes. One minute it's sunny—then, swish, a rainstorm. It's rather fascinating. There's no snow, though. I haven't seen any snow since—"

"Penny, please."

"I'm glad this house has a fireplace. I do adore a fire on a day like this. I curl up on the sofa and—"

"Penny!"

"No!" she cried. "I won't talk to you. I won't hear it all again—the lies about who you are, the macho declaration about how I belong to you. No, Cabe, I won't listen. I've had four months to discover who Penny Chapman is, and I like myself, like who I am. No one owns me. No one dictates the terms of my life. I want you to go and leave me alone. You can report back to my father that I'm fine. And you can tell him I'm staying right here. Alone. Do you understand? Alone."

"Penny, please listen to me," Cabe said, taking a step toward her.

She shook her head.

"No. I won't."

He continued slowly forward. "I love you, Penny. Every day of these four months has been a nightmare. I was so worried about you." She began to back up. "I've relived that scene in your father's office over and over. I'm so sorry, Penny. I never meant to hurt you. I just want to love you, to marry you and spend the rest of my life with you."

"No, no, no," she said, still retreating. "You don't understand. I can't do it. My father wanted to own Penelope; then you picked up where he left off. Lucky Penny was yours, your possession. Well, guess what? I'm not Penelope, and I'm not your Lucky Penny. I'm Penny, a new person, a blend of both Penelope and Lucky Penny. I'm myself, really myself, for the first time in my life. I'm protecting this new Penny from you, from Harold, from anyone who thinks he can own me. And you, Cabe—I don't even know who you are. There you stood in your fancy suit, with your hair so stylishly cut, and I didn't know who you were. You lied to me. Dammit, you even had business cards!" She backed into the wall with a thud.

Cabe closed the distance between them and planted his hands on either side of her head. He kept his body away from hers and looked down at her, his blue eyes flashing with anger.

"You're going to listen to me," he said, a pulse beating wildly at the base of his throat. "You owe me that much. You put me through a living hell these past four months."

"Owe you? I owe you nothing," she said. She pressed her hands against his chest and pushed, only to discover it was like trying to move a brick wall.

"Dammit," he said roughly. "You owe me *this*."

He grasped her head, holding it steady to receive

the full power of his punishing kiss. He took advantage of her whimper of protest by sliding his tongue between her lips, then plummeting it deep into her mouth.

No! Penny's mind screamed, but her heart whispered yes.

She slid her hands upward to circle his neck, inching her fingers into his damp, thick hair. She met his tongue boldly and heard a groan from deep in his chest. Feverishly, urgently, they drank of each other, their breathing raspy as their passions soared.

Cabe inched closer to her, needing to feel her softness pressed against him. He moved her away from the wall, one hand splayed across her back as he nestled her to him, letting her feel the extent of his heated arousal.

Then he stiffened. A message of enormous magnitude slammed into his passion-laden brain. He opened his eyes as he tore his mouth from hers and stared down at her flushed face. Her eyes were closed, her lips moist and swollen from his ravishing kisses.

"Dear God," he whispered.

"Hmmm?" she said dreamily, slowly lifting her lashes.

He moved back far enough to rivet his gaze on her stomach.

"You're pregnant."

Reality rocked Penny from the mist that had enveloped her, and she pushed Cabe's arms away. She pressed back against the wall, her eyes wide.

"I am not," she said, staring at the cleft in his chin. "I've just been eating a lot since I got here. Go away."

He lifted one hand and tentatively placed it on her stomach, an incredulous expression on his face. She shoved his hand away.

"That's rude," she said. "You can't go around plopping your big paw on people's stomachs. Go away."

"You're pregnant," he repeated. A slow smile crept onto his face, then widened into a grin. "You're pregnant with my baby! Hot damn, this is fantastic. We're going to have a baby!"

"We are not!" she yelled.

"Oh?" he said, still smiling. "You're into smuggling cantaloupes now, are you? There's a little round bulge under that tablecloth you're wearing, Penny Chapman."

"I do not bulge!"

"Shh, don't shout. You'll get our baby all up-tight."

"Go away," she said through clenched teeth.

"Ah, Penny." His smile faded as he cradled her face in his hands. "You know I'm not leaving you. I wasn't leaving you before I knew you were carrying my baby, and I'm sure as hell not leaving now. Weren't you going to tell me?"

"No," she whispered, tears filling her eyes.

"You weren't going to tell me about my own baby?" he asked, a flicker of pain crossing his features.

"They're mine. These babies are mine."

He opened his mouth to speak, but nothing came out. He cleared his throat and tried again.

"Babies?" he asked. "As in more than one baby? As in twins?"

Penny pushed past him and walked across the room, wiping her eyes as she went. She sank onto the sofa in front of the fire. Cabe followed to stand in front of her, his hands shoved into his back pockets.

"You really weren't going to tell me?" he asked, his voice raspy.

"No," she said, staring at her hands, clenched tightly together in her lap.

"Why?"

"Because I don't know who you are. The father of these babies is Cabe, a Cabe who doesn't really exist. These babies belong to the Penny I've become since I've been here. They have nothing to do with you."

"The hell they don't," he said in a voice so low, so menacing, that she stared wide-eyed at him. "Those babies are as much mine as they are yours."

"No."

"I can't believe this," he said, raking a hand through his hair. "You're still living in Alice's rabbit hole. You've created a fantasy world tailor-made to your specifications. Well, come back up to earth, Penny, because that ball game is over. I'm the father of those babies, and you know it. You can't keep me from my own children. Are you sure you're having twins?"

"Yes. I had a sonogram, and . . . Oh, Cabe, please go away. I just want to be left alone."

"I can't do that. Penny, I love you. It just blows my mind to think you weren't going to tell me about this. Didn't what we had together, what we shared, mean anything to you? Can you really dust me off this easily? We were so special, so wonderful to-gether."

"It wasn't real. You just said so yourself."

He hunkered down in front of her and covered her

hands with his. "In all its important aspects our relationship was real. You know it was. I realize I made a mistake by not telling you I owned my company, but it wasn't some devious plan to deceive you. I didn't want to run the risks of coming out of the rabbit hole, either. You'd accepted me as blue-collar Cabe. You'd said you were tired of businessmen in expensive suits, and I was scared to death to tell you about the other part of my life. Then things moved so damn fast, I just never had a chance to explain it all."

"But you showed up, didn't you? There you were in your fancy clothes, looking and sounding like a carbon copy of my father."

"Penny, please listen to me. I don't want to own you, possess you, smother you. I want you to be my wife, my equal partner, my best friend. I know your father and I went slightly nuts that day in his office, but I didn't mean it the way it sounded. You've got to believe me. Please forgive me for that day. Our entire future is at stake here. And the future of our babies."

"You keep telling me to listen to you, Cabe, but you won't listen to *me*. A million years ago we were Penny and Cabe, with no last names, pretending to be something we weren't. It's taken me all these months to discover who I really am. There's some of Penelope in me in my determination to succeed at what I do. And there's a portion of Lucky Penny, who knows how to laugh and how to cry. Blended together they're me, Penny, and you really don't know her, any more than I know who Cabe Malone is. Don't you see? We're strangers. We created these babies in another time and place that doesn't even exist."

"Those babies exist."

"Yes, they do, in the here and now. They're nestled within the Penny I've become. They're tiny, fragile little beings, Cabe. We can't build a relationship based on them. They're not strong enough to support us. They're not supposed to carry that kind of burden."

"We have more going for us than just the babies. I came here to get you, to take you home, to beg your forgiveness. I loved you before I knew you were pregnant, remember?"

"You love who I was, not who I am."

"Oh, hell," he said, pushing himself to his feet, "we just keep going in circles." He walked over to the fireplace and gripped the mantel with both hands as he stared into the leaping flames.

Penny gazed at his broad back and swallowed the lump in her throat. Cabe didn't understand, and her heart ached with the knowledge. They were strangers now, whether he was willing to admit it or not. They were no longer just Penny and Cabe, who had come together in ecstasy. They were Penny Chapman and Cabe Malone. Strangers. She loved the Cabe she had once known, just as he loved his Lucky Penny. And neither of those people was real.

But the babies were real, her mind echoed.

Yes, she thought wearily, Cabe was their father. He had the right to know his own children. She *had* created a scenario in her mind that wasn't realistic or fair. Cabe shouldn't be kept from his children. But what he had to face was that the babies were their only link. He, too, had to emerge from the rabbit hole and acknowledge the truth. They really didn't know each other.

"Cabe," she said softly, "I won't deny you the right to know your children. We'll set up a plan that's agreeable to us both."

"And us?" he asked, turning to face her. "What about us?"

"There is no 'us.' "

"I see. Fascinating," he said, a sarcastic edge to his voice. "I made love to you, I planted my seed in you, I created two human beings with you, but I don't really exist. I'm a father, but not a man? That's crazy. This whole thing is crazy."

"You're the one not facing facts, Cabe," she said, her voice rising.

His jaw tightened. "Don't say it again. Don't give me that bull about our being strangers."

"It's true!"

"Well," he said as he crossed his arms over his chest, "we'll just have to get to know each other, won't we?"

"What do you mean?"

"Just what I said. Okay, Miss Chapman, this calls for some compromises on both our parts. I'll concede the fact that we're strangers. As ridiculous as it is, I'll give you that one. In return, you'll come back to Detroit with me tomorrow."

"I certainly will not."

"Yes, you will. I have a company to run. You need to get to know me as the president and owner of that company. That can only be done in Detroit. This"—he swept his arm through the air— "is just another fantasy world. We apparently screw things up when we operate in fantasy worlds. Excuse the pun. We lose our identities, or whatever, in our fantasy worlds. Be ready to leave tomorrow. I'll make plane reservations."

"Now, just one minute, Cabe."

"Next on the agenda," he said, beginning to pace the floor. "I want to marry you immediately."

"No."

"Then we'll compromise. We'll live together in my apartment in Detroit."

"What?"

"Oh, not as lovers, but as the mother and father of that cantaloupe you're smuggling under your table-cloth. We'll be together every day, get to know each other, stop being strangers. Who knows? We may find out we don't even like each other. I've never lived with a woman before. Maybe you'll get on my nerves."

"Me? That's not a very nice thing to say."

"No more fantasies, my sweet. Everything is up-front now." He stopped pacing, his glance falling on her stomach. "No joke."

"Quit staring at my stomach. That is just so darn rude. Twins take up a lot of room. I can't help it if they're as big as a cantaloupe already."

"I think," he said quietly, "that you are absolutely beautiful. I wish I could see you naked, see the changes our babies have made in your body. A body, Penny, that I know as well as I know my own. You remember *my* body, don't you? How it feels, what happens to me when you get me so aroused, I'm ready to explode?"

"Cabe, don't," she said as desire thrummed deep within her.

"Don't remember how it was between us? Just forget the feel of your body tightening around me when I'm deep, so very deep, inside you? How can I erase all that from my mind? When we topple over the edge together it's like—"

"Stop it," she said, covering her ears with her hands.

He pulled her hands free and bent over to speak close to her lips. "Don't worry, Penny. I won't force myself on you while we're living together. I just want you to think about how it was between us."

"Why are you doing this?" she whispered.

He straightened and covered his heart with his hand. "Me? Hey, this is your harebrained scheme. We're strangers, says you. We don't know each other, says you. You're calling the shots here, not me. If this were my ball game we'd be married in a matter of days. But we'll do it your way. I'm going to call and make plane reservations. Where's the phone?"

"I—Oh, forget it," she said, shaking her head. "I'm too tired and confused. The phone is in the kitchen."

"You're tired? Don't you feel well? What in the hell were you doing out in the rain in your condition?"

She stood up. "Mr. Malone, I am going on record as of this moment as having said that if you ever again refer to this pregnancy as 'my condition,' I will personally break your nose."

"Oh, yeah?" he said, grinning. "I'm a little out-numbered. There're three of you."

"Keep it in mind. I'm going to go take a nap."

"Seriously, Penny," he said, his smile gone, "are you okay? What does your doctor say?"

"I'm healthy as a horse. My appetite is good, I walk every day, get plenty of fresh air. The babies are the size they should be, too."

"Good. We sure know exactly when they happened, don't we? I didn't do a damn thing to protect you."

"It's just as much my fault. No, I don't like the sound of that. Fault indicates blame, guilt. I'm not sorry about these babies. I want them very, very much."

"So do I," he said, trailing his thumb over her cheek. "I want our children, but I want us too."

"Cabe . . ."

"Okay, you don't have to spell it out for me again. We're compromising, right? We can go back to Detroit tomorrow. You probably have more stuff here than we can take on the plane, so just pack enough clothes for, say, a week, and we can send for the rest. So will you come with me tomorrow?"

"I guess. Yes, I'll go. I'm just not sure we should live together."

"It's the only way to find the answers we need."

"Yes, I suppose it is." She paused. "Oh, heavens, my father. Cabe, he'll never stand for this."

"Don't worry about it. You go take your nap, and we'll discuss the rest later. Go on."

"All right." She started to leave the room, but his voice stopped her.

"Penny?"

"Yes?" She looked back at him.

"I found you once in a half-built house; then I found you again in the middle of a rainstorm on a beach. Now we're searching for each other once more with this move to Detroit. I figure that the third time will be the charm. I'll find you, discover who you've become, who my Lucky Penny is now. And then . . . then I'll never, ever let you go again. I won't hold you with my hands, like a possession. I'll hold you with my love. Rest well."

She turned before he could see the tears brimming in her eyes.

"Oh, and, Penny?"

"Yes?" she said, keeping her back to him.

"I love the socks. They're first class. Those are Lucky Penny socks."

She laughed in spite of herself, then went into the bedroom. She slipped beneath the bedspread and sank onto the bed with a weary sigh.

She was exhausted, she realized. Her serene existence had once again been turned topsy-turvy by Cabe Malone. She was winging off to Detroit to set up housekeeping with a man she hardly knew! She had fallen in love with blue-collar Cabe, not business-card Cabe. She'd researched his company in the library in the town nearby, and knew he was a wealthy man. Her beautiful, shaggy-haired construction worker was probably a yuppie. Oh, Lord, who was Cabe Malone?

She rested her hands on her rounded stomach. The father of her children, that was who, she mused. But beyond that she didn't know. What would become of Penny Chapman and Cabe Malone together? She didn't know. Did they have a future as a couple, an "us," or were they to be no more than parents who shuffled their children back and forth between separate homes?

"Dear heaven," she whispered, "I just don't know."

She gave way to the fatigue that claimed her, and slept, oblivious to the rain still drumming on the roof. And oblivious to the two tears that slid silently down her cheeks.

Cabe made the plane reservations, then telephoned Harold and Martha. He told them each about Penny's pregnancy, her refusal to marry him, and their subsequent plan to return to Detroit. His tone of voice made it clear he was not soliciting opinions of the situation, and the parents were remarkably quiet.

After adding more logs to the fire, Cabe leaned his shoulder against the doorjamb of Penny's bedroom and stared at her as she slept peacefully.

Somehow, he thought fiercely, he was going to win that woman's love and trust. He needed to spend the rest of his life with her to erase the aching chill of loneliness of the last four months without her. Lord, how he loved her. And now she was carrying their babies. The future could hold so much happiness for all of them if she would let it.

He had to be patient, he told himself. He had to keep his damnable temper in control and give Penny time to learn how to believe in him again. Time? Hell, she'd already had four months! Four lousy months of his dying a little more each day. Wonderful. He was losing his temper already.

How, he wondered, was he going to live under the same roof with Penny and keep his hands off her?

His desire for her was nearly overwhelming already. Well, he'd just have to do it. They were starting from scratch, as strangers, according to Penny. Strangers, hell! He loved her!

She stirred on the bed, then stilled, curling her hand next to her cheek. Her hair was in tumbled disarray on the pillow, and Cabe felt his body tighten as he gazed at her beauty. Heated blood began to pound through his veins, and he pushed himself away from the doorjamb and headed for the kitchen.

"Yep, Malone," he muttered, "you've got a helluva road to go."

Seven

Penny awoke at six that evening to the aroma of frying bacon. She immediately realized that she was hungry—and that Cabe was there.

Cabe, she thought, closing her eyes again. She was returning to Detroit to live with the man! Was that insane? The way Cabe had presented his compromise, it had all made sense. No, it wasn't normal to live with a man so that the couple could "get to know each other." But then, it wasn't very ordinary to be four months pregnant with said man's twins. It was silly to consider a regular dating relationship, with Cabe calling on Tuesday to ask her out for Saturday. She and Cabe were certainly beyond that. He'd be dating her *and* the cantaloupe.

But living together? she asked herself. Well, they weren't exactly going to live together. There would be no lovemaking. Cabe wouldn't pull her into his arms. He wouldn't slowly remove her clothes and kiss every inch of her. He wouldn't stand before her in naked splendor, so tightly muscled, so tall and—

"Penny?"

She gasped, and sat bolt upright in bed, her hands flying to her flushed cheeks.

"What's wrong?" Cabe asked.

"You scared the living daylights out of me."

"You were expecting someone else?" he asked, smiling as he walked to the edge of the bed. "Did you sleep well?"

"Yes, thank you." She picked an imaginary thread off the spread. What would he see in her eyes, on her face, if she looked at him? she wondered frantically. Shame on her for having such wanton daydreams about their lovemaking, about becoming one with Cabe, about—

"Is there anything you need?"

"Oh-h-h," she moaned, pressing her hand to her forehead.

"Are you all right?" he asked anxiously, sitting down on the bed. "Penny? Talk to me."

"I'm all right," she said, staring at his chest. Her voice had squeaked. Squeaked, for crying out loud.

He gently cupped her chin and lifted it, forcing her to meet his gaze. "What is it?"

"I . . . um . . . I'm hungry. Yes, that's it. I need food. You'd be amazed how much food I consume to get the energy to smuggle this cantaloupe."

He turned on the bedside lamp and searched her face, his gaze lingering on her dark eyes. Penny told herself to move, not to fall prey to the mesmerizing depths of his blue eyes, but the message from her brain had no influence over her body. The room suddenly felt charged with sensuality, with crackling tension that seemed to be drawing them closer and closer. Then Cabe cleared his throat, breaking the eerie spell.

"Dinner is ready," he said, his voice husky. "Nothing fancy, just bacon and eggs."

"I adore bacon and eggs," Penny said, hearing the breathlessness in her own voice. "Bacon and eggs are superb."

Cabe slapped his hands on his thighs and pushed himself to his feet. "Right. So up and at 'em, kid. They won't taste good cold." He strode from the room.

"Right," Penny said, and drew a deep, steadying breath.

After shaking the wrinkles from her caftan and pulling a brush through her tangled hair, Penny joined him in the kitchen. They ate in silence for several minutes; then Cabe finally spoke.

"We have plane reservations for ten tomorrow morning."

"All right. I need to call my landlord and tell him I'm leaving. Did you speak with my father?"

"Yes, and my mother. I told them about the babies and that you're moving in with me."

"And?"

He shrugged. "No problem."

"My father didn't throw a fit? Come on, Cabe. I know better. He'd never approve of my living with a man. Unless, of course, he's disowned me because I'm pregnant."

"Penny, you probably won't believe this, but your father has changed. He was frantic while you were gone, didn't eat or sleep properly."

"Is he ill?"

"No, not exactly. I imagine he'll settle down now that we've found you. He's . . . wiser. He realizes what he has in you, and that because of his attitudes and actions, you ran. He also knows that I love you very much. He won't hassle us about our living arrangements. Harold and I have become close during the past four months. Closer, in fact, than my own father and I ever were."

"I suppose I should apologize for causing all of you such distress, but I had to leave, Cabe. I just couldn't handle it."

"What's done is done. I'm more concerned about the future. Want another glass of milk?"

"No, I've had plenty, thank you. I cleaned my plate like a good little girl, and it was delicious. I'll take care of the dishes, since you cooked."

"No, I'll do them."

"I'm not an invalid, Cabe. Why don't you take a cup of coffee into the living room?"

He hesitated, then finally nodded and left the kitchen. Penny loaded the dishwasher, scrubbed the frying pan, then wiped off the counters and table. When she entered the living room Cabe was slouched on the sofa, his long legs stretched out in front of him, and was staring into the fire. He'd turned out the lights, leaving the orange glow of the flames as the only luminescence. He appeared totally relaxed and half asleep. She sat down next to him, and he didn't turn his gaze from the fire.

"How's Holly?" she asked.

"Fine. Great," he said, smiling but not looking at her.

"And your mother?"

"She's doing okay."

"What about your father?"

He pushed himself up and leaned forward, resting his elbows on his knees and making a steeple of his fingers as he continued to stare into the fire.

"He died two months ago."

Penny felt as though a cold hand had clutched her heart, and she had difficulty breathing for a moment.

"I'm so sorry," she said, placing her hand on his back. "What happened?"

"He had another stroke. We rushed him to the hospital, and he lived for a few hours. He was conscious part of the time. He managed to tell my mother how much he loved her. I'm glad for her about that. Lord knows she always took a back seat to the law practice and Jason."

"And you, Cabe? Did you speak with your father?"

He sighed, a weary-sounding sigh. "I knew he was dying, Penny. So I gave him the only gift of good-bye I had to offer him. I—I pretended I was Jason."

"Oh, Cabe," she whispered.

"My father was tired, confused, and he didn't question it. I said, 'It's me, Dad, Jase. Quit messin' around so we can get back to work.' Jase would have said something like that. He took my hand and squeezed it; then he smiled. He smiled at Jason. He said, 'I love you, son.' He—" Cabe stopped speaking as emotion choked off his words. "He never said those words to me in my entire life. Only—only to Jason. But he smiled, Penny, and then he died. I'm glad I did it for him. I had nothing else to give him."

Tears spilled onto Penny's cheeks as she rested

her head on Cabe's broad back. She wanted to hold him, comfort him, erase the hurt that his father had caused him.

How very much it must have cost Cabe, she realized, to hear those words, meant for Jason. What a price Cabe had paid to bring a moment of happiness to a dying man. What an incredibly beautiful human being was Cabe Malone. And what a cold, unfeeling father Matthew had been.

"My children," Cabe said, his voice ringing with determination, "will be loved. My children will be accepted for who they are, just as they are. They'll choose their own paths, and I'll wish them luck. And I will tell them, over and over and over again, that I love them."

"Oh, Cabe," Penny said, her voice cracking.

"Hey," he said. He turned and gathered her into his arms, pressing her head to his shoulder. "Shh, don't cry. I didn't mean to upset you. It's just so easy to talk to you, Penny. It seems so right, and feels so damn good, to let go of what's been bottled up inside me. I shouldn't have dumped it on you. I didn't mean to make you cry."

She lifted her head to look at him through a mist of tears. "I'm crying *for* you, not because of you. Don't ever be afraid to talk to me, Cabe. Please don't start shutting me out. We shared, right from the beginning, when we were Penny and Cabe, with no last names. That was one of the things that made us so special. Remember?"

"Of course I remember. I remember every minute of our time together." He cupped her face in his hands and drew his thumbs through the streaks of tears on her cheeks. "Every detail of every minute," he murmured, then lowered his lips to hers.

So sweet, so soft, Penny thought dreamily, parting her lips to receive his tongue. So Cabe.

She lifted her arms around his neck as he dropped his hands to her back. Memories of another time and place flooded over her. Memories of Meadow View and what she had shared there with Cabe. Memories of kisses like this, that tasted like this, that ignited her passion, just like this. It had been Cabe then, and it was Cabe now.

The kiss became urgent as his hands roamed restlessly over her back, pressing her closer and crushing her breasts against his chest. A soft moan caught in her throat. The sensual sound caused Cabe to shudder with desire, and his hold on her tightened. He tore his lips from hers, then trailed hot, nibbling kisses down her throat.

"Oh, Cabe," she whispered, trembling in his arms.

"I want you, Penny," he said, his voice raspy. "I ache from wanting you. It's been so long, and I missed you so damn much."

"Yes, I . . ." She paused to draw a steadying breath. "I want you too. We'll be Penny and Cabe. Just Lucky Penny and Cabe. Nothing else is important. Nothing."

She felt him stiffen, felt his muscles quiver as he strove for control, felt him move away from her, leaving her cold and wanting.

"Cabe?"

He lunged to his feet and walked to the fireplace, his back to her. He gripped the mantel with such force, his knuckles turned white, and she saw the shudder that ripped through his body.

"Cabe?"

"Dammit, no!" He spun around to face her, his hands curled into tight fists at his sides. "I won't do it, Penny. I won't function only in the world at the end of the rabbit hole. *I won't play games!* Everything else *does* matter. It matters that I'm Cabe *Malone* and you're Penny *Chapman*. We *do* have last names, and lives beyond the bed we'd share. It matters that you're carrying my babies. They may have been created in the midst of one of our fantasies, but they're real—*we're* real. We don't have time for make-believe. Do you know what time it is? It's half past forever. We're at a crossroads, deciding the rest of our lives. We'll either have it all, together, or share only the lives of our children. But I can't, I won't, make love with you as only Penny and Cabe, with no last names."

Penny wrapped her arms around herself in a protective gesture. "Yes, of course you're right," she whispered. "I just . . . I just wanted you so much, and . . . I'm sorry."

Cabe muttered an expletive, then planted his hands on his hips as he stared at the ceiling. When he felt in control again, he looked at her.

"Don't ever," he said softly, "be sorry that you want me. But there's too much at stake here to play games." He started across the room. "I'm going for a walk."

"Cabe, it's still raining."

"It'll take the place of a cold shower. I have to get out of here for a while, Penny, before I do something I'll regret. You'd better go to bed. We have a big day tomorrow."

"I just got up."

"Cantaloupes need a lot of rest. Put the babies to bed, and you go with them. Oh, hell, I don't know. I really have to get out of here." He left the room.

"But it's so cold and dark, and"—she heard the kitchen door slam—"and stuff. Oh, darn." Well, fine, she thought. Let him go stomp along the beach and freeze his gorgeous tush off; she didn't care. He had certainly picked a crummy time to be logical. Couldn't he have faced reality after they'd made love? Dammit, she wanted that man.

Still, she knew Cabe had been right to call a halt, and that made her mad too. Construction-worker Cabe would have just jumped on her bones. But business-card Cabe avoided rabbit holes like the plague and was level-headed and noble.

Fully aware that she was pouting, and muttering a few less-than-ladylike words, Penny went into the bedroom and began to pack for the trip the next day.

When Cabe entered the kitchen two hours later, he told himself for the umpteenth time that he wasn't too bright. Only an idiot set off for a walk in a cold, dreary rain without even the benefit of a jacket. And only an idiot refused to make love with the woman he loved.

"You're an idiot, Malone," he mumbled, heading down the hall to the second bedroom. He wasn't a total idiot, though, he decided as he stripped off his clothes. A medium idiot. The walk in the rain was stupid. Staying out of Penny's bed was not.

He was shivering from head to toe when he stepped into the shower and turned the water on full force, closing his eyes to savor the warmth.

He'd done the right thing, and he knew it. His body didn't know it, but his mind did. What he had said was true—there was no time to play games.

After his shower he literally dove into bed. He pulled the blankets up to his nose and decided he was cold again. Penny was in the next room. He could crawl into bed with her, wrap himself around her, and absorb her body heat. It would be strictly therapeutic, of course. The remedy for his freezing self. And he was such a liar, it was ridiculous. Oh, he'd warm up, all right. He'd be so damn hot so damn fast that he'd move over her, then into her, in one motion. Oh, sweet heaven, what ecstasy it would be to feel her honeyed heat closing around him once more, tighter and tighter, until . . .

He moaned as his body responded to his thoughts. "Oh, Lord, I'm dying."

He pushed the image of Penny from his mind. Then, instead of counting sheep, he mentally recited, in alphabetical order, every swear word he had ever heard.

The morning produced clear blue skies, a rather subdued Penny, and an aching-all-over Cabe.

"Don't you feel well?" Penny asked as they ate breakfast at the kitchen table.

"No."

"What's wrong?"

"I don't feel well," he said gruffly.

"Would you care to be more precise?"

"My body hurts. All of it."

"From walking in the rain last night, I'll bet," she said. "I didn't think it was a very good idea at the time. You should be in bed. We could postpone the trip another day, and I'll fix you chicken soup."

"No. We're going home."

"Home," she repeated, staring into her coffee cup. "It sounds so simple, but it really isn't."

"Nope," Cabe said, squeezing the bridge of his nose, "but the way we're doing this is the only plan on the drawing board. Are you about ready to go?"

"Yes."

He began to massage his temples. "I like that whatever-it-is you're wearing. It's cute."

"This, sir," she said, peering down at her blue jumper and blue-and-white striped sweater, "is your standard maternity jumper. I would have added knee socks, but I wasn't sure the people on the plane could handle such a gorgeous overall picture."

He smiled. "Cute as a button."

"Cabe, think about it. I'm in maternity clothes at four months. I'm going to look like a close relative of a whale before this is over."

"Hey," he said, trapping her hand with his on the top of the table, "you'll be beautiful. Know why? Because there are two miracles inside you. They're part you, part me, and they're people. Little tiny people. It blows my mind. They have fingers, toes, noses, the works. You won't look like a whale; you'll look like a woman. A woman doing what a man can only be in awe of. Believe it, Penny. You'll be beautiful through the whole nine months."

"Oh-h-h," she said, her bottom lip trembling, "that was so sweet."

"So you're going to cry?" he asked, eyeing her warily.

"No." She sniffled. "I guess not. I never know, though, what's going to set me off. They had a parade here on New Year's Day, with high school bands, and horses pulling these wagons, and I wept through the whole thing."

He chuckled. "That's a privilege of your . . . um . . ."

"Cabe Malone!"

"I didn't say it!" he said, raising his hands. "I didn't say 'your condition.' Did you hear me say it? No, you did not. Don't hit me. I feel lousy enough as it is."

"Your cheeks are flushed," she said. "You have the flu."

"No," he said dryly. "You're kidding. Golly, gee whiz, do you really think I have the flu?"

"You're crabby when you're sick. I'm making a note of that. Did you take some aspirin?"

"Yeah," he said. "Let's hit the road."

"You should be resting, Cabe."

"I will when we get home," he said, standing up. He began to cough as he left the kitchen.

Home, Penny mentally repeated as she followed him from the room. Did he live in an apartment, a condominium, a house? And would she and Cabe ever really share a dwelling that was truly a home because it had that special ingredient of love? Would Penny Chapman and Cabe Malone find what Penny and Cabe, with no last names, had shared? She hoped so. With every breath in her body she hoped so.

Cabe slept during the flight to Detroit, surfacing only when coughing spells jolted him awake. He told Penny to spend her time looking out the window so that she wouldn't breathe the germs cluttering up his air space. Their landing in Detroit was delayed by a raging snowstorm that had airport traffic stacked high into the heavens.

Cabe had left his car at the airport, but driving on the snow-slicked streets was hazardous and slow. Cabe's cough worsened, as did his mood, and sweat beaded his brow despite his grumblings that he was freezing to death.

When Penny had offered to drive, he had shot her a look that clearly indicated that he might have the flu but he wasn't insane, thank you very much. After that, Penny kept silent. She was tired, hungry, and longed for the solace of her own apartment—which a friend of hers was looking after—rather than facing the momentous event of moving in with Cabe. All she wanted to do was get something to eat, then crawl into bed and sleep.

"Aachoo!"

The volume of Cabe's sneeze caused her to look at him worriedly as he turned into an underground garage. He whipped the car into a parking place.

"You have *got* to start drinking liquids and taking aspirin," she said. "It's straight to bed for you, Cabe Malone."

"No can do." He turned off the ignition and got out of the car.

Penny met him at the trunk. "Why can't you go to bed?" she asked, glaring up at him.

He grinned at her. "I'm a mere mortal man. Take pity on me, woman. All you think about is getting me into bed."

"Very funny."

He laughed and pulled their five suitcases from the trunk. Penny carried the two smaller ones as Cabe juggled the remainder.

"I probably shouldn't have brought all of this stuff," she said. "I really can't get into most of my clothes."

"Let's go," Cabe said, nodding toward the elevator. "You'll have to buy a bunch more of those cute outfits, because of the cantaloupe."

"The way the babies are growing, I'll have graduated to smuggling a watermelon pretty quickly here."

"And you'll be beautiful," he said quietly.

She smiled as they entered the elevator.

"Push sixteen," he said.

She did as instructed, and the doors swished closed. As the elevator started upward, she looked at Cabe.

"Why can't you go to bed?" she asked.

"Penny, Penny, shame on you."

"Stop it," she said, smiling. "Just give me a straight answer."

"I cannot go to bed because as soon as I step into my living room—excuse me, *our* living room—I have to call my office and have a bid package delivered to me for my review. The bid goes in first thing tomorrow morning, and no bid leaves Malone Construction without my signature and my eagle eye having checked every detail. Got it?"

"Oh." She frowned. "Is it a big job?"

"Yep. About thirty million dollars' worth of condos."

"Cabe, that will be a big package. It will take you hours to check."

The doors opened, and she stepped out of the elevator. Cabe was right on her heels.

"Hey," he said, "how do you know how long it's going to take me to go over the bid?"

"Which way do we go?" she asked, glancing around.

"Left. Sixteen thirty-two."

"Come on. Those suitcases have got to be getting heavy." She started down the carpeted hallway.

"Answer the question," he said, falling into step beside her. "How do you know?"

"Penelope knows," she said, looking at the numbers on the doors they passed. "I reviewed bid packages all the time at Chapman and Chapman. I checked a proposal once that was as thick as a telephone book."

"No kidding," he said, surprise evident in his voice. "You're good, huh?"

"One of the best, buster. Here it is. Where's your key?"

"Well, shucks and darn, it's in my pocket, and my hands are full. Guess you'll have to dig in there and get it. Please don't take liberties with me. I'm a sensitive person."

"Cute, Cabe," she said, setting her suitcases down

with a thud. "You're just too cute for words. Which pocket?"

"Right hand side of my jeans. In the front. Next to the zipper. See that bulge? That's my—"

"Cabe!"

"Keys! What did you think I meant?" he asked, all innocence.

"Put a cork in it," she said, glowering at him.

She slid her fingers into the tight pocket and immediately felt Cabe tense. Adopting his innocent expression, she wiggled her fingers back and forth, and slowly, oh, so slowly downward.

"Oh, good Lord," he muttered, sucking in his breath.

"Problem?" she asked, batting her eyes at him.

"Just get the damn keys," he said gruffly.

Mission accomplished, Penny inserted the key in the lock and pushed the door open. After retrieving the suitcases, she stepped into the apartment.

"It's lovely," she said, absently setting the suitcases down on the thick, dark brown carpet. The furnishings were of the finest quality and the decor was masculine, but not to the extent that a woman would feel uncomfortable. He had used earth tones, oranges and yellows, brown and tan, to create a warm and inviting atmosphere. "I really like this, Cabe."

"I'm glad," he said, setting his own luggage down.

"My apartment is about this size," she said, running her hand along the back of a nubby, oatmeal-colored sofa, "but it's . . . I don't know. It's cold. It looks like a store display. This is marvelous."

"Good. I'd like to pull you into my arms and kiss

you. A 'welcome home' kiss, an 'I'm glad you're here with me' kiss, but I won't, because I'm a walking disease. Look around all you want. I have to call my office."

"Yes, all right," she said, already peering at the books on a floor-to-ceiling bookshelf.

While Cabe was on the phone she wandered down the hall, smiling. This was business-card Cabe's apartment, she thought, and she was seeing a part of him she hadn't known existed. There were some obviously valuable pieces of art hanging on the wall, but she knew he'd bought the paintings because he liked them, not for their monetary worth. Cabe worked hard for his money, and reaped the rewards of his labors. And to think she had once thought he squandered his paycheck and had to live with his parents.

The guest room—her room, she supposed—was good-sized. Against one wall was a bookcase holding books, toys, dolls, and games, and she surmised that Holly used this room when she visited her uncle Cabe.

The master bedroom was enormous, and as Penny stood staring at the king-sized bed, her smile faded. The spread was rich tones of brown, tan, and orange in a diamond pattern, and the colors were carried over into the bathroom beyond the bedroom.

Cabe's bed, she thought. Cabe's bed, where she wouldn't sleep. She'd be a room away, keeping company with Holly's toys. Lord, this was absurd. She was carrying the man's babies, for heaven's sake. She and Cabe had shared the greatest intimacy a man and woman could share. But that was before.

She wouldn't be with Cabe in this bed until they knew, accepted, and loved the person each really was. No more fantasies. No more trips down Alice's rabbit hole.

With a sigh Penny retraced her steps, and found Cabe in the large kitchen. He was stirring something in a pan on the stove as he rubbed his forehead with his other hand.

"Dinner?" she asked, walking to his side.

"Yeah. Soup and sandwiches. I'll get more stuff in tomorrow."

"I'll serve this up, Cabe. You sit down at the table. You really look awful."

"I don't have the energy to argue the point," he said, and collapsed into a chair at the table.

Within a few minutes Penny had the simple meal on the table, and Cabe swallowed two aspirin before starting to eat.

"When are you planning on seeing your parents?" he asked.

"Tomorrow, I guess."

"You don't look too thrilled about it."

"I'm not."

"Harold has changed, Penny. I don't know your mother that well, but I can honestly say that your father is a different man from the one I first met."

"We'll see. Now that I'm back, he could very well slip into his old mode of behavior. And speaking of my father, I've been thinking about my job. I can't picture myself working at Chapman and Chapman again, but I do need to do something. And you should get the chance to see Penelope doing her thing."

"I think that's a good idea. You shouldn't work too hard, though. Maybe you could go part-time."

"Possibly. I was considering free-lancing as an investment analyst when I was in Florida, but then I discovered I was pregnant, and concentrated on my health, to get the babies off to a good start. I did volunteer work at the library instead, helping cross-reference a backlog of books. Besides . . ." Her voice trailed off.

"Besides?" he prompted.

She fiddled with her sandwich. "I guess I knew that my father would find me. Every day that went by was like hours stolen for myself, to discover myself. Yes, I knew he'd come after me."

"And me? Didn't you realize that I would be searching for you? If Harold hadn't been around to hire detectives, I would have. Lord, Penny, you heard me say that day in Harold's office that I loved you and wanted to marry you. Did you believe I'd just shrug it off, forget you'd ever existed?"

"I didn't know what you might do, Cabe," she said, meeting his gaze. "You became a stranger that day you arrived at Chapman and Chapman. I still don't know who you really are."

"Which is why we're here."

"Yes."

"Fair enough. We're starting over. We'll—" A ringing sound interrupted him. "There's the doorbell. It's probably the messenger with the papers from the office."

He left the kitchen and returned minutes later, a thick folder in his hand. He sat back down at the table and flipped the folder open to the first page.

"Wonderful," he said. "My eyes don't even focus properly. Checking this thing out should be a good trick."

Penny took a deep breath. "Cabe, we could do it together."

"What?"

"I'd do the whole thing for you, but I know you wouldn't be comfortable with that. We could at least do it together in half the time. Then you could get the bed rest you need."

He folded his arms over his chest and rocked onto the back legs of his chair as he studied her. Minutes passed, and Penny's heart thundered.

"I think," he said finally, thudding the chair back onto all four legs, "that it's time I got to know the Penelope part of you. We'll check the bid together."

"Thank you, Cabe," she said, smiling. "Penelope *is* a part of me, and it's so important that you know who she is."

"You're right," he said, nodding. "And I suppose you'll say you have to get to know business-card Cabe too."

"Yes."

He stood up. "The thing is, in my case the bottom line is the same. I'm Cabe Malone. I'm a man, pure and simple. I'm the father of your children, and the man who loves you more than life itself. That, my Lucky Penny, is never going to change." He started toward the door. "Let's get to work on the bid."

Eight

At a little past midnight, Cabe tugged off his shoes, socks, jeans, and briefs, then drew his sweater up over his head. As he dropped it onto the floor, he was amazed that his aching arms hadn't come off in the process. He was, as he'd decided hours before, a dying man.

He crawled beneath the blankets on the bed and groaned. Then groaned again. He hurt. There wasn't one inch of him that didn't hurt, including his teeth and hair. The flu was the pits, he hated it, and he needed some tender, lovin' care.

And, he thought, pulling the blankets higher, he sure as hell wasn't going to get it from that Penelope! When Penny gave full rein to Penelope, she didn't mess around. Penelope, he'd discovered at around nine o'clock, had a mind like a steel trap. At ten he'd become totally in awe of her eye for detail. At eleven he'd mentally labeled her a slave driver.

So, okay, he admitted to himself, between eleven and twelve he'd moaned and groaned, coughed louder than necessary, and asked for time out to make his will. That was no reason for Prissy Penelope to tell him he was behaving the way Holly might. Dammit, he was sick!

And Penelope Chapman was the most intelligent, efficient woman he had ever met.

She absolutely blew his mind. And scared him to death. Would Penelope give up the challenge available to her at Chapman and Chapman to step into Penny's roles of wife and mother? She could work part time, he supposed, but the demands made by twins were endless. The world he offered Penny was far removed from the one Penelope existed in. How did he know if he and the babies could make her happy? Ask her? Hell, he wouldn't know what to say to Penelope unless it had to do with a spread sheet. He didn't know who she was!

"Damn," he mumbled.

Then, as if an invisible hand had flicked a switch, Cabe closed his eyes and fell deeply asleep.

In the guest room Penny told herself to relax and get some sleep. She lay rigid and stiff on the bed and squeezed her eyes tightly closed. Thirty seconds later her eyes popped back open.

It had been an enlightening evening, she thought. Even as sick as Cabe was, he'd been thorough and efficient, missing no detail and cutting no corners as they checked the bid, which was one of the finest, most complete packages she'd ever seen. He'd been all business—when he wasn't moaning like a wounded cow, of course. Business-card Cabe was quite a man.

What had he thought of Penelope? she wondered. When they'd finished working he'd mumbled his good night and shuffled off to bed. Poor baby. He was so sick. But surely tomorrow he would comment on her expertise, thank her for her help. Then would he suggest that she work with him again for Malone Construction?

She rolled onto her side and rested her hand on her stomach. "I'll just have to wait and see what the morning brings. Good night, cantaloupe," she whispered, and closed her eyes and drifted off to sleep.

Cabe stood in front of the mirror to straighten his tie, then leaned closer to inspect his reflection.

He'd lived through the night, which was, he decided, a positive sign. He actually felt pretty good, considering he'd been at death's door and hadn't received one iota of tender, lovin' care. He could smell freshly made coffee, which meant Penny was up and in the kitchen. He was stalling, had changed ties three times for no reason, and he felt like an idiot.

But, dammit, he thought, combing his hair yet again, what if Penny was still in her Penelope mode? He didn't want to discuss bid packages over breakfast, but he wouldn't know what else to say to her. He wanted Penny to be Penny! So he simply wouldn't acknowledge the Penelope part of her so early in the morning. Lord, this whole thing was getting nuts.

He started toward the door, then retraced his steps to the mirror to practice several pleasant, good-morning smiles. He could pull this off. He hoped.

"Good morning," Cabe sang out as he entered the kitchen. "Coffee smells great."

"You're chipper," Penny said, smiling at him. "Feeling better?"

"Top-notch," he said as he poured himself a mug of coffee.

"I'm glad. Shall I cook you some breakfast?"

"No, this is fine. I have to hustle." He sat down at the table. "Did you sleep well?"

"Yes," she said, sitting opposite him, holding her own mug.

"That's good." He picked up his spoon and began to tap out a rhythm on the table, giving the concert his undivided attention.

He hadn't looked at her, Penny thought, frowning slightly. He was looking everywhere but at her. Maybe she should nudge him into the subject of the bid, which would lead to the subject of Penelope, which would give her a clue as to where Cabe's head was.

"So!" she said brightly. "The big bid goes in this morning."

"Yep," he said, adding the whacking of a knife to his serenade.

"Well, I certainly wish you good luck."

"Thanks." He leaned closer to his instruments as he increased the tempo, his head bobbing up and down to the beat.

Penny scowled. "Do you have to do that?"

"Great way to start the day. Gets the juices flowing."

"I'm happy for your juices," she said dryly, "but you're giving me a headache."

"Oh." He dropped the knife and spoon onto the table. "Sorry. Well, I gotta shove off." He stood up. "See ya."

"Cabe—"

He kissed her quickly on the forehead. "Have a good one. 'Bye." He strode from the room.

"Have a good one?" she repeated, blinking. "Yuppies say that." Darn, she fumed, Cabe was acting thoroughly weird. What had happened to thanking her for her help with the bid? And what had happened to being awed by Penelope's intelligence and expertise? And what had happened to his suggesting she work with him again? All she'd gotten was a peck on the forehead after an ear-splitting knife-and-spoon concert. What on earth was the matter with that man?

Three hours later, Penny stood outside the closed door to Harold Chapman's office. She drew a deep breath, then squared her shoulders, turned the knob, and stepped inside.

"Hello, Harold," she said as she closed the door behind her.

Her father's head snapped up, and an instant later he was on his feet and coming around the desk toward her.

He looked terrible, she thought. Too tired and too

thin. She'd done this to him with her exodus to Florida.

He stopped in front of her and lifted his arms as though to hug her. He hesitated, though, and dropped his arms to his sides.

"Hello, Penelope," he said, his voice unnaturally hoarse. "No, it's Penny now, isn't it? You'll have to be patient with me until I get used to that. You're looking well."

"I'm looking pregnant," she said, attempting a smile. It failed.

"Yes, I know. Cabe told me. Both your mother and I are very excited about the prospect of becoming grandparents."

"I beg your pardon?"

"I guess you'll think I'm being foolish, but . . . well . . ." He swept his arm in the direction of the sofa against the far wall.

Penny's eyes widened. "Oh, my gosh," she said.

Sitting side by side on the sofa were two of the biggest stuffed panda bears she had ever seen. They had red bows around their necks and silly grins on their faces. Tears filled her eyes, and she kept her back to her father as she struggled to regain her composure. She didn't know what to do or say. She didn't want to be there!

Suddenly she thought of Cabe and the heartbreaking story he'd told of pretending to be Jason for his dying father. It was all he'd had to give Matthew Malone, Cabe had said. Matthew had died without ever acknowledging Cabe as a worthwhile son. They would never have another chance to create a bond between them. They'd never have another chance to say, "I love you."

But Harold Chapman was alive, she thought. He was reaching out to her, tentatively, cautiously. He was saying so much by calling her Penny and by allowing two enormous stuffed animals to sit in his neat and proper office. And there she stood with her back to him, closing him out.

She swallowed past the lump in her throat and turned slowly to face her father. He was watching her anxiously.

"The pandas are adorable," she said, tears misting her eyes again. "They're really very cute, and—Oh, Daddy, I'm so sorry I caused you such worry when I ran away. I was being really selfish, thinking only of myself. I hurt so many people, and I never intended to do that. I just couldn't be here any more. I couldn't breathe. Can you forgive me, Daddy? Please?"

"Oh, my Penelope." He opened his arms to her, making no attempt to stop the tears that streamed down his face. "You haven't called me Daddy since the day you left for college."

She rushed into his arms, sobbing openly as he held her tightly.

"I'm the one asking for your forgiveness," he said, his voice choked with emotion. "I lost touch with humanity somewhere along the line. It took your leaving to show me what I'd done to you, and to myself, Cabe, bless him, let me ramble on for hours about the mistakes I'd made. He's a fine man, Penel— Penny. Oh, my darling child, welcome home."

"I love you, Daddy," Penny said, moving back to

smile at him through her tears. "I think . . . I think you're going to make a wonderful grandfather."

"Darn tootin', I am. I was never much of a father to you, and I regret that more than I can say. I was so afraid I'd lost you forever, that you wouldn't allow me close to you and Cabe and those babies."

"We're going to be a family, all of us." She paused and turned to look at the pandas again. "No, maybe that isn't true. Cabe and I are in a type of limbo. We're half past forever. I know that doesn't make sense, but it's hard to explain."

"He loves you, Penny."

"Yes," she said, looking at Harold again, "but . . . Oh, I just can't discuss this right now or I'll cry for hours."

"I won't pry. But I want you to know I'm here if you need me. I do love you, you know."

"Oh-h-h," she wailed, "don't be so nice to me."

He chuckled. "You remind me of your mother when she was pregnant with you. I remember the time I told her I'd had the oil changed in her car, and she clung to my neck and wept for twenty minutes."

"Really?" Penny said, managing a wobbly smile.

"Really." He patted her hand. "Now, why don't we phone your mother and have her meet us for lunch? We have a lot to celebrate."

"That sounds lovely. Also, I'd like to come back to work for a while, if that's all right with you."

"Of course it is. You set your own hours; don't wear yourself out."

"Thank you for everything."

"No, Penny. *I* thank *you*. And as for Cabe . . . Well, I guess all I can say is, listen to your heart."

"Yes," she said softly, "yes, I will."

When Cabe arrived home at six o'clock the air was filled with a peculiar odor. Suddenly a piercing scream reverberated from the kitchen.

"Good Lord," he said, taking off at a dead run. "Penny!"

In the kitchen he came to a screeching halt, grabbing the counter to help stop his forward flight and to keep from sliding into the puddle of broken eggs on the floor.

"Oh-h-h," Penny cried, covering her face with her hands, "I can't stand it."

Cabe stepped over the eggs and gently pulled her hands away. She looked up at him, tears streaming down her face.

"Are you hurt?" he asked anxiously.

"No," she said, shaking her head. "I was . . . Then the . . . I wanted to . . . But the . . . Oh-h-h." The tears started again.

He gathered her close and patted her on the back. "I see. Could you run that by me a little slower? Maybe fill in the blanks a bit?"

Penny snuggled closer to his warmth, inhaling his special scent and feeling his steely muscles beneath the material of his suit and shirt. She wiggled closer yet, and felt Cabe suck in his breath.

"Penny?" he said, his voice sounding rather strangled. "Did the eggs attack you? Talk to me, sweetheart."

"Hmmm?" she said dreamily.

"Penny!"

"Oh!" Her head popped up, and she stepped back, brushing the tears from her cheeks. "I was going to surprise you with a special dinner, but nothing went right, because I burned the broccoli, the roast is just sitting in the oven like a lump, and I was going to make a cake, but I killed the eggs, and—"

He kissed her.

He slid one hand to the nape of her neck, the other to the small of her back, hauled her to him, and kissed her. It was an incredible kiss, a toe-curling, powerful kiss that seemed to steal the very breath from her body. His tongue delved deep into her mouth, and she met it with her own. They tasted and touched and savored as she leaned against him, going nearly limp in his arms. The kiss was Cabe, and Penny wanted it to go on forever.

Cabe drank of Penny's sweetness like a thirsty man finding lifesaving water on a barren desert. His manhood strained against his trousers. He could feel her full breasts pressed to his chest, and the gentle swell of her belly where his babies lay safe within her, being nurtured by all that she was. He felt a tightness in his throat as emotions piled one onto the next, and he continued to hold and kiss the only woman he had ever loved.

At last he lifted his head. "I love you," he said, then gripped her shoulders and tenderly set her away from him. "Even if you are an egg killer," he added. Her bottom lip began to tremble. "Oh, geez, I'm kidding! Look, it was a nice thought, the dinner, really nice. Tell you what. We'll go out to eat to celebrate the fact that Malone Construction got the contract for that bid."

"You did?" she said, a smile instantly on her face. "Oh, Cabe, that's wonderful."

"The word came in just before I left the office. The job is ours. I really appreciate your help in checking that bid last night. You're a first-rate—that is, Penelope is a top-notch . . . Anyway, we'll celebrate. I'll clean up the dead eggs, shower, and change. Then we'll go. You put your feet up, for now."

"No, I'll help you."

"No!" he said sharply. Her eyes widened in surprise. "I'll do it," he said, his tone softening. "Please, go relax in the living room. Go on."

"Well, all right," she said hesitantly, "but I did make this mess, you know."

"Don't worry about it."

She walked to the door, then turned to look at him again. He smiled and nodded, then averted his eyes as he shrugged out of his jacket. She left the kitchen with slow, dragging steps.

Cabe released a pent-up rush of air and stared at the ceiling for a long time, his jaw clenched so tightly that his teeth ached.

He couldn't do this! He couldn't weigh and measure everything he said and did around Penny for fear that Penelope would take front-row center and stay there. Penny had said she was now a blend of Penelope and Lucky Penny, but how did he know that was true? And, dammit, she'd never said that she loved him. Not even once had she said those words he ached to hear.

With a sigh that seemed to rip at his soul, he began to clean up the kitchen.

Penny washed her face and brushed her hair, then smoothed the material of her new, kelly green maternity dress. She sat down on the sofa and stared at the door to the kitchen.

Something was wrong with Cabe—she knew it— and she didn't want to think about it. There had been a desperate quality to his kiss. It was as though he'd been fighting an inner war of some kind— wanting to kiss her, yet not wanting to. When he'd told her to leave the kitchen, she'd virtually felt the tension emanating from his tightly coiled body. Sexual frustration, pure and simple? No, it was more than that. Much more. Something was definitely very, very wrong.

The babies moved within her, feeling like tiny birds or butterflies fluttering their gentle wings. She pressed her hand to her stomach in a protective gesture.

"We'll be fine, cantaloupe," she whispered. "Whatever is wrong with Cabe, we'll face it, and we'll be fine. I think. I hope. Oh, dear."

When Cabe appeared in the living room a short time later, she gazed at him anxiously. He busied himself unbuttoning his shirt and pulling it free of his pants. Her gaze skimmed over the enticing view of his bare chest. Then her eyes searched his face for a clue as to what he was thinking.

"All clean," he said, looking somewhere over the top of her head. "The roast wasn't cooking because the oven wasn't on. I wrapped the meat up and stuck it in the refrigerator. I'll go shower now."

"Cabe," she said softly, "what's wrong?"

"Nothing," he said, starting across the room.

"Cabe, please."

"I said it's nothing," he repeated, then strode from the room.

Penny blinked away her tears and sighed.

The restaurant was busy, and Penny and Cabe waited in the cocktail lounge for a table to become available. Within moments a stout man in his fifties approached Cabe and shook his hand vigorously. Cabe introduced the man to Penny as J. T. Smith.

"Damn good to see you, Cabe," J.T. said. "We're overdue for me to beat you at handball."

Oh, sure, Penny thought dryly. Cabe would run circles around this guy.

"You certainly whip my butt," Cabe said, smiling.

No way, Penny thought. If Cabe lost to this guy, he lost on purpose. Why?

"I'm about to open for bids on my new hotel on an invitation-only basis," J.T. said. "Are you in, Cabe?"

"I'm in."

That was why! Business-card Cabe played the courting game with prospective clients. She'd witnessed it all the time at Chapman and Chapman and had accepted it as a natural part of the business world. But it was an aspect of Cabe she'd never seen before, and for some unknown reason it was disturbing.

The two men chatted for a few more minutes. Then

Cabe's name was called, indicating their table was ready.

Penny didn't speak until after they'd ordered their meal. "You let J. T. Smith beat you at handball?" she asked.

Cabe shrugged. "It puffs up his ego, keeps him happy. You know how it is."

"Yes, but I guess I thought you wouldn't . . . Never mind."

"Wouldn't what?"

"Play the game, the courting game. Do you enjoy that part of being business-card Cabe?"

"Not particularly," he said, his jaw tightening, "but it's necessary. And as Penelope, you know that."

"I came here tonight as Penny."

"Well, excuse me all to hell. What am I supposed to do, keep a scorecard so I know who you are at any given moment? Look, I'm an honest businessman. I don't take bribes or kickbacks or use faulty materials when no one is watching. But, yes, I wine and dine clients, play the game, as you so astutely put it. I don't intend to apologize for that. You're a fine one to talk, Penny. While you were being Penelope, working on my bid, I could have passed out cold and you wouldn't have noticed."

"Don't be absurd."

"Can we give this a rest?" he asked, frowning deeply. "I'd like to enjoy my dinner, if that's all right with you."

"Fine," she said stiffly.

But they enjoyed neither their meal nor the tense, silent drive home. And they didn't enjoy the moment when they turned to face each other in the middle of Cabe's living room.

"I—I guess I'll go to bed," Penny said softly. "I told my father I'd be in the office in the morning. Thank you for the dinner. Good night, Cabe."

"Good night," he said, shoving his hands into his pockets. She didn't like business-card Cabe, he thought. She didn't like that Cabe and had never said she loved blue-collar Cabe. Dear Lord, was he going to lose his Penny?

"Yes, well, good night," she said, starting across the room. He thought Penelope was cold and unfeeling, she realized as she left the room. A computerized robot, or something. Penelope was efficient, that was all, and was only a part of her. Didn't Cabe understand that? Oh, what was happening to them?

It was nearly eight o'clock the next evening when Penny let herself into Cabe's apartment. He pushed himself slowly up off the sofa and crossed his arms over his chest.

"Nice of you to drop by," he said in a dangerously quiet voice.

"I'm sorry I'm so late, Cabe, but I—"

"Let me guess," he interrupted, raising a hand to silence her. "Penelope got so involved in her work, she lost all track of time. You didn't think about people, either, or you would have called to let me know you were going to be late, instead of leaving me to sit here and worry."

"I did phone. The line was busy."

"I wasn't on the—Oh, yeah, I was. I spoke briefly with J. T. Smith."

"Oh? Were you setting up a date for handball so you could lose for the benefit of his ego?"

"Don't stand in judgment of how I conduct my business, Penny."

"And don't you stand in judgment of me," she retorted. "For your information, Mr. Malone, I left the office at five o'clock sharp. I stopped at Hudson's to browse through the baby department to look at all the clothes. When I came out, I had a flat tire. I called you, and the line was busy, so I phoned the auto club. Now, I'd like to know why you assumed I was being Penelope because I was late."

"You've been Penelope for a long time," he shouted. "What if you decide you like that world best after all? What happens then?"

"Dammit, Cabe, this isn't a contest to see which Penny wins or which Cabe wins. We're supposed to be accepting all we are as complete people, every aspect of ourselves."

"But you don't like the fact that business-card Cabe loses a lousy handball game to please a client."

She sighed. "I understand why you do it, and there's nothing wrong with it. It just caught me off guard, that's all."

"Lord," he said, staring up at the ceiling. "I can't believe this." He looked at her again. "Listen to us, Penny. We're dissecting each other as if we're looking into a microscope. Who is she now? Who is he now? Peneleope? Penny? Lucky Penny? Blue-collar Cabe? Business-card Cabe? Then we squint into the lens and decide if we approve. I can't live this way."

"What do you mean?" she asked, feeling a chill course through her.

"I know it was my idea," he said, his voice strained, "but it was a mistake. It isn't going to work. We're not going to find any answers living together like this. I think it would be better if we had some space between us to sort things through."

"Do you want me to leave?" she asked.

"Yes," he said, even as his mind and heart screamed no. He had to let her go, give her time to think, to decide if she loved him, all of him. "But you can't just disappear again. I couldn't handle that. You wouldn't do that to me, would you?"

Tears closed her throat, and she could only shake her head.

"Do you understand why we have to do this?" he asked.

Yes, she thought dismally, she understood. Cabe needed time to think, to decide how he felt about Penelope, about Lucky Penny, about the woman she had become.

She nodded.

"Where—where would you like to go?" he asked quietly.

She cleared her throat, willing herself to speak without bursting into tears. "Meadow View. I'll go to Aunt Beth's house, in Meadow View."

"All right. I'll drive you up in the morning."

"I'd prefer to go alone, Cabe. I'll need my car once I'm there, anyway."

"Then I'll follow you, make sure you get there safely."

"No."

"Dammit, I . . ." He paused. "Yeah, okay. Look, I've been going to Meadow View every weekend to visit Holly. Could I see you this weekend when I'm there?"

"Yes, of course. I'll go to my apartment now and pack. I'll leave from there in the morning."

"You want to go now?"

"I think it would be best."

They gazed at each other, their eyes filled with sadness. Thoughts tumbled through their minds, but weren't spoken. Love burned within them, but wasn't declared.

There was only silence.

Nine

Early Saturday afternoon, Penny wandered aimlessly through her aunt Beth's house. Since arriving on Thursday, she had cleaned the house from top to bottom. Her efforts to push Cabe from her mind had failed, and tears were always near the surface.

Lord, she was tired of crying.

She walked to the living-room window and stared outside, not seeing the light layer of snow on the ground or the pale blue sky overhead. Not seeing anything but the image of Cabe Malone in her mind's eye.

The scene that had taken place in his apartment haunted her. The remembrance caused an ache in her heart, not because of the harsh words spoken, but more from the oppressive silence that had created an unbreachable wall between her and Cabe.

She leaned her forehead against the cold windowpane and sighed. "Oh, Cabe," she whispered, "what are you thinking? Are you still at half past forever?"

She had to get out for a while, she decided, before she went crazy. Ever since she got up that morning she'd been watching the clock, wondering if Cabe had arrived in Meadow View yet, trying to guess when he might drive up in front of the house. He'd step into the living room and . . . say what? Do what? Tell her what? Yes, she was definitely going for a walk before she stretched her jangled nerves any further.

The air was clear, crisp, and cold, and she buried her hands in the pockets of her coat. She inhaled deeply, immediately reaffirming in her mind that the walk was a splendid idea.

She really liked Meadow View, she mused as she strolled along with no particular destination in mind. It was just the right size, had fine schools, plenty of shopping facilities, a hospital, and none of the grueling pace and madness of Detroit.

She could live here as Penny, and somehow she knew the people of Meadow View would accept her as she was, never expecting her to be something else. She could laugh here and cry here. She could do free-lance work for Detroit companies. She could raise her babies here, in this town that had long ago given welcome and peace to her aunt Beth.

Her babies? her mind repeated. No, they weren't just hers. Cabe was their father. Cabe was her lover. Cabe was her love, her *raison d'être*, the center of her existence. Oh, she realized now she was complete within herself, a whole and total woman, but Cabe added that warmth, that glow within her that made her smiles real and her laughter come from a fountain of bubbling happiness inside of her. Lord, how she loved him.

Penny stopped, her eyes widening as she realized how far she had walked while buried so deep in her thoughts. She was standing in front of the half-built house where she had first met Cabe. Except now, the house wasn't half-built. Like the others, it appeared to be completely finished. In the distance she could see smoke curling from the chimneys of three of the houses, and cars were parked in the drive-ways, indicating families already were in residence. The other houses had "For Sale" signs on the front lawns.

Her gaze shifted again to the house she'd fled to that day so long ago. There were no curtains on the windows, nor was there any evidence that someone lived there. But neither was there a "For Sale" sign out front. Perhaps it was sold and the people simply hadn't moved in yet. Just a peek, she told herself. She'd take just a quick peek in the window to see how the living room looked finished.

She approached the house tentatively, definitely feeling like a thief in the night as she climbed the three steps and stood on the porch.

"Oh, how lovely," she said, lifting her hand to the carved front door. She traced the intricate scroll-work of the dark wood, then gasped as the door opened under her feathery touch.

She glanced around, a tingle of excitement sweeping through her. She shouldn't go farther, she knew it, but, oh, the urge to step inside that house just once more was irresistible. This was the house where she had met her Cabe.

Hardly breathing, she inched inside, then closed the door behind her with a quiet click. To her amazement the house was toasty-warm, and she could hear the hum of the furnace that was supplying the welcoming heat. Thick cocoa-colored carpet was on the floor and covered the stairs leading to the second floor. Her gaze swept over the oyster-colored walls and the stone fireplace, topped by a gleaming wood mantel.

There was no furniture in the large room, but her imagination quickly supplied sofas and chairs. There were dark wood end tables, and lamps with softly glowing light . . . and a playpen for the babies.

There were toys scattered on the carpet. Dolls and trucks and building blocks. Cabe would sit with Holly and the twins in front of a roaring fire, and they'd build towers of blocks. The babies would squeal in delight, then knock the blocks over so their patient daddy could stack them up once again.

Penny smiled, thoroughly engrossed in her fantasy. Let's see, she pondered. Where was she while Cabe was entertaining the children? Well, since this was a make-believe scenario, she was in the kitchen baking wonderful cookies. She was an absolute whiz of a cook, and wouldn't even come close to killing a poor, defenseless egg.

Penny blinked; then surprise flashed through her as the empty room came back into focus. It had all been so real, so vivid, that she'd actually heard the sound of laughter and smelled the aroma of cinnamon.

It had been a marvelous journey down Alice's rabbit hole, but she really had to leave. The house was obviously about to be occupied, and with her luck, the owners would drive up right now and catch her trespassing.

But . . . Her gaze shifted to the stairs. Just a glimpse, she thought. Just a glimpse of that room, that special room, where Cabe had come upon her when she'd been crying for Aunt Beth. She'd dash upstairs, have a look, then go. If the wild thudding of her heart meant anything, she was not cut out for a life of crime.

She walked across the large room, delighting in the feel of the rich carpet beneath her feet, and started up the stairs, her heartbeat thundering in her ears. At the top she glanced around quickly, then tiptoed to the room she sought. She stopped at the doorway, and her mouth dropped open.

Cabe was sitting on the floor with his back against the wall, in the exact spot she'd been on that day he'd found her.

Oh, stop it, Penny told herself. Cabe wasn't really there. Her imagination was working overtime. He wasn't there, with his long legs, encased in faded jeans, stretched out in front of him. His sheepskin jacket wasn't next to him on the carpet, nor was he wearing a gray sweater that emphasized his wide shoulders and muscled chest. That wasn't a real-life Cabe, with his head leaned back against the wall, his eyes closed, and lines of fatigue etched on his handsome face. She was being ridiculous. Cabe wasn't there.

He coughed.

Penny gasped and took a step backward.

He slouched a little lower. His even and steady breathing seemed to hint that he was asleep.

She squeezed her eyes tightly closed, counted to ten, then opened them again.

Good Lord, Cabe was there! He really was!

Now what? she wondered. Should she sneak back out, leave him alone, wait for him to come to her at Aunt Beth's? No, now, just a minute. She couldn't, wouldn't, believe that Cabe's being in *this* room, in that exact spot on the floor, was a coincidence. He had come for the memories, just as she had. He had come to relive that first meeting, that special, rare, wondrous reaching out between Penny and Cabe, with no last names. It had all started right there, and Cabe knew that. Their journey toward forever had begun within this room.

Penny smiled. It was a smile of everlasting love. She unbuttoned her coat and slipped out of it, placing it on the floor just inside the door. One hand slid into a pocket of her dress, closing around her treasure, her momento of that first day. She walked quietly into the room and eased herself down next to Cabe.

Then she simply looked at him, every beautiful inch of him, her heart nearly bursting with love.

As if sensing her presence, he slowly opened his eyes and turned his head to meet her unwavering gaze.

"Your mother," she said softly, "taught you never to leave the house without a clean handkerchief in your pocket. My mother"— she drew the handkerchief from her pocket—"taught me always to return the things I borrow."

Cabe glanced at the handkerchief she extended toward him, then looked at her face again. She couldn't read the expression on his face. He shifted his gaze once more to her hand and covered it with his. He rested their hands on the carpet between them, then leaned his head back against the wall and closed his eyes.

Neither spoke.

It was so quiet, Penny was certain Cabe would hear the wild thudding of her heart. She gazed at his large, strong hand and remembered how it had felt on her breasts, on her entire body, the callused fingers infinitely gentle as they roamed over her soft skin. His lips would follow, igniting within her a burning, passionate need for him, that only he could quell.

As one they would soar to their private place of splendor, then drift back. It would be a union not only of bodies, but of souls as well. A joining so complete, it would be almost impossible to tell where one left off and the other began.

Oh, such personal depths they had shared, she thought. She couldn't lose this man, this extension of herself. He was a gift to be treasured and cherished, to be fought for if need be. It was time to fight for Cabe. She wanted all of him, blue-collar Cabe and business-card Cabe, for they were one and the same. Whether he was wearing jeans and swinging a hammer or dressed in a three-piece suit and negotiating a multimillion-dollar deal, he had pride and integrity.

Oh, how foolish she'd been. How complicated she'd made their lives, for no reason. Cabe Malone was not a stranger. She knew all of him now, and loved all of him.

She turned her head to look at his face, but he hadn't moved or opened his eyes. To a casual observer, she supposed, he would appear to be a totally relaxed man enjoying a catnap. But *she* saw the muscle tickling in his jaw. *She* felt the slowly increasing pressure of his hand on hers as the tension built within him.

"Cabe," she said quietly, "I know you're not asleep. I'd like to talk to you."

"No," he said, not opening his eyes.

"No, you're not asleep, or no, I can't talk to you?"

He sighed and opened his eyes, staring down at their entwined hands. "I was hoping that if I kept my eyes closed, I wouldn't have to hear what you want to say. But there's nowhere to run and hide, is there? No more rabbit holes. I was going to come to your house, but I stopped here first. I wanted to be here, in this room, where I first found my Lucky Penny."

"Cabe, I—"

"All right," he said. "I'll shut up. Go ahead. Talk. Tell me that the only link between us is our babies. What's the plan? I get to see them every other weekend or something?"

"No, I—"

"Wonderful," he went on, with a snort of disgust. "I'll see Holly one weekend, the twins the next. That's a helluva life. Do I sound like I'm feeling sorry for myself? Well, I am. I decided to indulge in a little self-pity simply because I wanted to. Yeah. Poor Cabe. I didn't ask for a lot, didn't set my sights so high that they were unrealistic. All I wanted was for my woman to love me as much as I love her. I wanted my family around me and—"

"Cabe, I love you."

"Want to know something?" he rambled on. "This is my house. I couldn't bring myself to sell it after it was finished. I put the carpet down weeks ago; then I waited for you. I sat here today thinking how Lucky Penny cried in this room, then laughed, with me. We were together. I looked around and thought that Penelope would click on her superbrain and know what we should do about making the house baby-safe for the twins."

"I do love you, Cabe, with all my heart."

"Penelope would handle that baby-safety stuff like a pro," he continued, apparently unaware that she had spoken. "And Lucky Penny? Well, see, Lucky Penny knows about rabbit holes, and when we needed one, just for the two of us, we'd get a baby-sitter and whiz right down that old hole for some stolen hours alone. And then there's Penny. She's part Lucky Penny and part Penelope, but she's herself, new, whole, a wonderful blend of both, and—"

"Dammit, Cabe, shut up!"

"—and I love her so much," he said, sounding totally miserable. "I really love her, but she doesn't—"

"I love you, you idiot," Penny said. She got to her feet and glared down at him, her hands planted on her hips. "If you interrupt me again, I'm going to break your gorgeous nose."

"Huh?"

"Listen up, Malone. I kept quiet earlier because I wasn't sure how you felt about who I've become. I was giving you time and space to think things through."

"What in the hell for?" he asked, scrambling to his feet and glowering at her. "I told you all along that I loved you."

"Shut up!"

He snapped his mouth closed.

"You knew I was confused, Cabe. I was convinced that we were strangers, that what Penny and Cabe, with no last names, had shared wasn't enough to build a lifetime on. But I was wrong. The first voice, the first messages, from my heart held all the answers, but I was too frightened to listen."

"Penny—"

"Shhh."

"Right."

"Blue-collar Cabe and business-card Cabe aren't worlds apart, two separate entities. Your values and beliefs, your honesty and integrity, are the same. You're not a stranger to me, Cabe. You haven't been from the day we met right here in this room. And, oh, God, I love you so much. I want us to be together with our family, with the twins, and Holly, and the panda bears, and—and I'll learn how to make cinnamon cookies if you'll play with the building blocks, and . . . Oh, dear heaven, say something."

"What panda bears?"

"That's it," she said, spinning around. "I've had it. I'm leaving." She stomped toward the door. "I might as well be talking to a fence post."

He caught up with her and stopped her flight by scooting in front of her and gripping her shoulders.

"You love me?" he asked, knowing his smile was growing bigger by the second. "All of me? Blue-collar Cabe, business-card Cabe? Cabe, your lover, your man, the father of your babies?"

"And Cabe, the son," she said, tears filling her eyes, "and the brother. Yes, Cabe, I love you. With all my heart, with all that I am as Lucky Penny, Penelope, and Penny, I love you."

"Oh, thank God," he said, and pulled her close, his arms holding her tightly.

A tremor swept through him as he buried his face in the fragrant cloud of her hair and clung to her as if he'd never let her go again. She wrapped her arms around his waist and leaned against him, savoring his warmth, his strength.

They were home.

They were standing in the empty house Cabe had helped create with his own hands. Together they would add the ingredient of love to turn it into a home.

Cabe drew in a deep breath, then slowly lifted his head. He cradled Penny's face in trembling hands and made no attempt to conceal the tears glistening in his eyes.

"I love you," he said, his voice hoarse with emotion. "I love you, Penny."

"And I love you."

He kissed her. It was a kiss so soft and sensuous, Penny felt like the most precious piece of crystal ever created by a master's hand. Cabe stroked away her tears with his thumbs as he continued to brush his lips over hers, nipping, fluttering, suckling just enough to start the heat of desire pulsing deep within her. Her knees began to tremble, and she clutched his arms for support.

"Oh, Cabe," she whispered.

"I want you, Penny," he murmured, his lips against hers. "I want to make love to you here, in our room, in our home."

"Yes."

He captured her mouth in the searing kiss that she had been yearning for, as his hands moved to the zipper at the back of her dress.

"Cabe," she said as he slowly drew the zipper down, "I look different from when we made love before."

"I want to see our cantaloupe," he said, slipping the dress from her shoulders. "Those are *our* babies. Yours and mine." The dress fell to the floor, and his heated gaze swept over her. "Oh, Penny. You are the most exquisite, the most beautiful woman I've ever seen." He rested his hand on her stomach. "I can't believe this. They're in there, all safe and warm, growing. There're two little tiny people in there, Penny."

"I know," she said, smiling. "Believe me, I know."

His gaze shifted upward to the new fullness of her breasts, and he swallowed heavily. He lifted his hand, then hesitated, searching her face for reassurance. She looked directly into his eyes as she undid the front clasp of her bra and dropped the lacy garment to the floor as she stepped out of her shoes.

"Love me, Cabe," she whispered.

With a groan he lifted her into his arms and took possession of her mouth with a fiery kiss. Then he carried her to the center of the room and laid her gently in a halo of sunlight that streamed through the window. He stood again and quickly shed his clothes.

Penny's breath caught in her throat as she gazed up at his magnificent body. He stood over her, strong and powerful, his manhood a bold announcement of his love for her. He was Cabe, naked before her, offering all that he was. She lifted her arms to welcome him into her embrace.

He dropped to his knees beside her and drew her panties down her legs and away. He stretched out on the floor, resting on his arm as his gaze inched over her, blazing a path of desire wherever it went.

"So beautiful," he said, his voice husky as he leaned over her. "So womanly and lovely. Mine."

She sank her fingers into his thick tawny hair and urged his mouth onto hers, meeting his tongue, hearing the groan that rumbled up from his chest. His hand sought her breast, and his thumb trailed over the nipple until it was a taut button. The kiss went on and on, growing urgent, frenzied, hungry.

His hand moved lower, skimming gently over the swell of her stomach, down to her thighs, then to the moist heat between. She gasped in pleasure, and he drew her nipple deep into his mouth, suckling with a rhythm that matched the stroking of his fingers.

"Oh, Cabe," she said, her voice trembling. "Please. I need you. I want you so much."

His only response was to move to her other breast, loving it until she cried out.

"Tell me," he said. "Tell me again that you love me."

"I do. I love you more than I can even say. I—Oh! Please, Cabe. Now. Please!"

He gazed at her flushed face. "I don't want to hurt you, Penny."

"You won't."

"The babies—"

"—are fine."

"It's been so long. I don't know if I can hold back, Penny, to give you pleasure and—"

"Oh-h-h, you talk too much," she said with a moan.

"Oh, yeah?" He smiled as he moved over her. "You like action, huh?"

"Oh, you'd better believe it," she said, cupping his face in her hands. "Come to me, Cabe. Take me all the way to forever."

And he did.

He came to her with all that he was, sheathing himself in all that she was. They were one, complete. Half past forever was left far, far behind, never again to be revisited. They soared ever higher, seeking ecstasy, then bursting upon the forever shore in all its splendor.

"Cabe!"

"I love you, Penny. Lord, how I love you."

He shifted off her and tucked her close to his side. She snuggled against him with a contented sigh. He sifted his fingers through her hair, watching the silken strands change color in the glow of the sunlight. A lovely, peaceful silence fell over the room.

"Penny?" he said finally.

"Yes?"

"Will you marry me?"

She tilted her head back to look at him, a gentle smile on her face.

"Yes."

"Don't you want to think it over?"

"No."

"Oh. Well, that's good. No, this isn't fair. We need to talk first."

"Okay," she said with a little shrug. "Talk."

"There's Holly, you know. I'm coming to you with a daughter. She's adorable, of course, but she can be a bit sassy sometimes. Not rotten, but . . . I love her, Penny. I want her to have a real family again. My mother has been super, but it's time for me to fulfill my promise to Jason and Karen. And then there's this house. See, I really would like to live in Meadow View, raise our children here. I can delegate authority at the company, and I wouldn't have to go to Detroit that much. You could do some Penelope work for Malone Construction if you wanted to. I guess we have a lot of things to cover."

"Yes."

"Well, we'll take them one at a time."

"No. What I mean is, yes, I'll marry you. And yes, of course Holly will be our daughter. Yes, I adore this house and Meadow View, I'll give Malone Construction the honor of my expertise on occasion, and . . . What else? Did I leave anything out? Oh! I love you and I want to spend the rest of my life with you. There. How's that?"

"Perfect," he said, lowering his lips toward hers, "except for one little item."

"Which is?" she asked, and flicked her tongue along his bottom lip.

"Do we really own some panda bears?"

"I'll explain all about the pandas," she said, trailing one finger down his chest, then lower and lower. . . . "Later."

And it *was* much later before Penny and Cabe reluctantly dressed and left the house that would soon become the Malone home. They walked back to Aunt Beth's hand in hand, delighting in the big, wet, lacy snowflakes that had begun to fall.

Meadow View was being transformed into a winter fairyland of beauty, Penny thought. It wasn't a make-believe world, but a real one. It was Penny and Cabe, having traveled far to earn the right to stake their claim on forever. Together.

Epilogue

Cabe opened the front door and stepped inside his house. The aroma of burnt cookies immediately reached him, and he chuckled softly as he shrugged out of his suit jacket.

"Hi, Uncle Cabe," Holly said, running into the living room.

"Hi, cute person," he said, tugging on one of her pigtails. "It smells like we're having ice cream for dessert again, huh?"

"It wasn't my fault," Penny said, coming into the room. "I went to check on *your* sons, and while I was gone, the cookies burned."

"Oh, I see," Cabe said, laughing as he pulled her into his arms. "It was Jason and Jeff's fault."

"Sure," she said, matching his smile. "How was Detroit?"

"Busy, big, boring. It's good to be home. By the

way, we're all set for the weekend. My mother will baby-sit the troops, and we are gone."

"Heavenly, but I wish you'd tell me where we're going."

"Down a custom-made rabbit hole, my Lucky Penny, where no one exists but Penny and Cabe, with no last names."

"I love you so much, Cabe," she whispered.

"And I love you," he said, lowering his lips to hers.

"And the cookies are burning!" Holly yelled.

"Oh!" Penny gasped, then spun around and ran toward the kitchen. Cabe was right on her heels.

As darkness settled over the town of Meadow View, the joyous sound of laughter echoed through the home of Cabe and Penny Malone. A home filled to overflowing with love.

THE EDITOR'S CORNER

I AM DELIGHTED TO WELCOME KATE HARTSON AS YOUR AUTHOR OF THIS MONTH'S EDITOR'S CORNER, AND TO LET YOU KNOW THAT NORA ROBERTS'S NEXT SIZZLING ROMANTIC SUSPENSE NOVEL—**SACRED SINS**—WILL COME OUT NEXT MONTH.

HAPPY HOLIDAYS!

Carolyn Nichols

I'm delighted to have joined the LOVESWEPT team as Senior Editor to work on these fabulous romances, and I'm glad to be writing the Editor's Corner this month so that I can say *hi* to all of you.

Isn't it a treat having six LOVESWEPT books every month? We never have to be without a LOVESWEPT in the bedroom, den, or purse. And now there are enough of these luscious stories to last through the month!

Soon we'll be rushing into the holiday season, full of sharing and good cheer. We have some special LOVESWEPT books to share—our holiday gifts to you!

RAINBOW RYDER, LOVESWEPT #222, by Linda Hampton, is a gift of excitement, as our respectable heroine, Kathryn Elizabeth Asbury, a pillar of the community, finds herself attracted to Ryder Malone, a wildly handsome rogue who has a penchant for riding motorcycles. Kathryn's orderly life is shaken by Ryder, who isn't quite what he appears to be. She fights hard for control

(continued)

but really can't resist this wild and free-spirited "King of the Road." Then she makes a thrilling discovery—and falling hard doesn't hurt a bit. **RAINBOW RYDER** is sure to be one of your favorites, but don't stop reading, we have five more LOVESWEPT GIFTS for you. . . .

Diamonds are the gift in Glenna McReynolds's **THIEVES IN THE NIGHT,** LOVESWEPT #223—how appropriate for the holiday season! Our heroine, Chantal Cochard, is an ex-jewel thief forced out of retirement when her family's prize diamond necklace shows up around some other woman's neck. DIAMONDS may be a girl's best friend, but they're not her lover. That's better left to well-built, sexy men like our hero, Jaz Peterson. Once Chantal invites him into her Aspen hideaway, she quickly learns that love is the most precious jewel of all!

Witty Linda Cajio's gift to us is **DOUBLE DEALING,** LOVESWEPT #224, a story of childhood dreams and adult surrender. Our heroine, Rae Varkely, mistress of a fabulous estate, is forced into a position where she simply has to kidnap Jed Waters. She makes a ransom demand, but our hero refuses to be released! Making demands of his own, he turns the tables on Rae, who can't help but pay with her heart. Still she has to protect her property from Jed's plans for development. But Jed has no intention of destroying anything—he only wants to build a strong relationship with the mistress of the manor.

A new book from Kay Hooper is always a gift, but **ZACH'S LAW,** LOVESWEPT #225, is an especially wonderful one. As the tale continues of those incredible men who work for Joshua Logan (and who indirectly fall out of SERENA'S WEB), we meet petite Teddy Tyler stranded on a deserted mountain road. Zach Steele, a strong, silent type who frightens Teddy because he ignites such strong desire in her, is her rescuer . . . then her sweet jailer . . . and the captive of her love. But Hagen's got his claws into Zach, there's mayhem on the horizon, and there's Zach's own past to confront before true love can win out!

(continued)

Sara Orwig's **OUT OF A MIST,** LOVESWEPT #226, is a gift of desire, as Millie and Ken are reunited after a brief but unforgettable encounter. Ken is on the run from the law, and Millie discovers him wounded and hiding in her closet. Of course, she knows he's done nothing wrong and she lets him stay with her until they can clear his name. But the longer he stays, the more he finds a place in her heart. Millie blossoms in Ken's embrace, but Ken won't settle for just passion—his desire is the lasting kind!

Our final romantic gift for you is a wonderful new book by Patt Buchiester called **TWO ROADS,** LOVESWEPT #227. This moving book is a story of healing: Nicole Piccolo is recovering from a broken leg and a broken heart, trying to forget Clay Masters, the man who promised her *forever* and then disappeared from her life. When Clay reappears a year later, the wounds are opened again, but Clay is determined to show Nicole that he never meant to leave and his heart has always been hers. When the healing is complete, they begin again with no pain to mar the exquisite pleasure of being in love.

Enjoy our gifts to you, sent with love and good cheer from your LOVESWEPT authors and editors!

Kate Hartson

Kate Hartson
  Editor
LOVESWEPT
Bantam Books, Inc.
666 Fifth Avenue
New York, NY 10103

NEW!

Handsome Book Covers Specially Designed To Fit Loveswept Books

Our new French Calf Vinyl book covers come in a set of three great colors— royal blue, scarlet red and kachina green.

Each 7" × 9½" book cover has two deep vertical pockets, a handy sewn-in bookmark, and is soil and scratch resistant.

To order your set, use the form below.

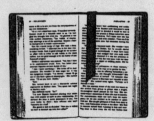